THE GIRL INSIDE

Young Christy Frederickson had scarcely absorbed the shock of losing her mother when her father was killed in an automobile accident. In the terrible days that followed, an incident that Christy might ordinarily have taken in stride triggers a suicide attempt.

Luckily, at this point, Christy is befriended by a young lawyer and his wife, but just as she is regaining her balance, tragedy hits again. Painfully, Christy comes to the realization that the frightened girl inside her must grow up before she will ever be able to handle her life successfully.

"A very human story. . . . Christina is a real teenager, facing problems very real to today's youth and not always solving them—until she is able to face a few facts about herself. A sensitive portrayal."

—Albuquerque (N.M.) *Tribune*

THE GIRL INSIDE

Jeannette Eyerly

A BERKLEY HIGHLAND BOOK
PUBLISHED BY
BERKLEY PUBLISHING CORPORATION

The quote on page 134 is from "Stopping by Woods on a Snowy Evening" from YOU COME TOO by Robert Frost. Copyright 1923 by Holt, Rinehart and Winston, Inc. Copyright 1951 by Robert Frost. Reprinted by permission of Holt, Rinehart and Winston, Inc.

Published by arrangement with J. B. Lippincott Co.

SBN 425-01928-4

BERKLEY HIGHLAND BOOKS are published by Berkley Publishing Corporation 200 Madison Avenue New York, N.Y. 10016

BERKLEY HIGHLAND BOOKS ® TM 758,135

Printed in the United States of America

BERKLEY HIGHLAND EDITION, NOVEMBER, 1970
2nd Printing, July, 1971
3rd Printing, April, 1972
4th Printing, July, 1972
5th Printing, August, 1972
6th Printing, November, 1972
7th Printing, December, 1972

CONTENTS

CHAPTER ONE

"Property City Hospital"

From the too big seersucker robe with the words "Property City Hospital" stamped across the back, to her peaked face wisped about with hair straight and fine and white as ocean sand, everything about her was pitiful and forlorn.

Miss Marple, the nurse who had brought her from the ward, squeezed her hand encouragingly. "A psychiatrist is just like any other doctor," Miss Marple said. "All he wants is to make you well."

The girl shook her head as if she could make the words go away and two tears rolled unevenly down her cheeks.

The door before which the two stood, opened. From within a man's voice said kindly, "Don't be afraid."

The girl moved one step forward. The voice spoke again. "Everyone here is your friend."

The paper scuffs on her small cold feet made a dry, crackling sound as she shuffled into the room. With a brief, anguished glance she looked about her. Several of the people she did recognize. The social worker who'd asked her all the questions when she was well enough to talk; the woman who gave her the tests; the young intern with the unpronounceable name full of z's and s's.

But now these half-familiar encouraging faces were no help. Fear made it almost impossible for her to move toward the chair facing the desk at which the doctor sat. Yet his eyes behind the dark-rimmed glasses with the shiny lenses seemed to pull her toward him.

He opened the manila folder that lay before him. "I'm Dr. Brandon," he said. "And you are Christina Marianne Frederickson." He smiled. "A very pretty name, but rather long for every day. What do your friends call you?"

A small, bitter laugh bounced off the walls of a cavern deep inside her. She had no friends. She had had friends in Spring Valley. Their house on Nightingale Hill had teemed with friends. But that was *before*. One by one, after her mother died, they seemed to disappear. And since her father had brought her to live with Aunt Henriette she had had no friends at all.

The doctor was listening, waiting for her to speak as if time would last forever. But it was not until he phrased the question once again that her whispered answer came. "Christy. My friends . . . my father . . . called me that."

"Then I shall call you Christy, too," said Dr. Brandon matter-of-factly.

"*Christina*," the girl said so flatly that the doctor smiled.

"Christina, then." He turned over a loose sheet of paper within the file. "Dr. Zabrowsky says you're feeling better. Your temperature is normal, your lung X-rays clear. It won't be long before you'll be able to go—that soon you'll be able to leave us."

Swiftly, she flicked a glance upward from red-rimmed eyes. He had caught himself just in time. Although he had not said "go home," he still had given himself away. He knew that she had no real home. It was all written out there on the paper before him, just as she'd told it to the social worker. He also knew that she had no friends. She despised him for knowing these truths about her, yet at the same time she wanted to fling herself into his arms and be comforted.

Dr. Brandon, elbows resting on the desk, made a steeple of his fingers. He was looking at her in a calm, clear way. He said, "Tell me what happened, if you can."

"I . . . I don't know. I . . . can't remember." Now the room seemed to be spinning around and around and all the people in it. She wove her cold fingers into a lattice work in her lap and stared at them as if they were the only stable things in a twirling universe. "I . . . I was frightened."

"Because, after your father died, you had no real relatives of your own?"

Her latticed fingers made a dry, whispering sound. "That was worst. There were other things."

"What other things?"

She let her head sink into the hollow between her hunched shoulders. Though the room seemed to have righted itself, now it was the silence that was growing. Even the sounds of summer outside the open window no longer could be heard.

Dr. Brandon still was waiting, listening as he had before.

"I . . . I was afraid of Leo Cole."

"Leo Cole?" Dr. Brandon shuffled the papers before him, looked up with a shadow of irritation on his face. "I don't see any mention of him here."

A woman scurried forward from the back of the room. "I'm sorry, but I didn't include him in the file, though I should have, I know." She leaned farther over the desk and continued in an audible whisper in the direction of Dr. Brandon's ear. "He rooms with Mrs. Zengler. A nephew, I believe. He happened to hear Christina the night she left the house and thinking something might be wrong, he followed her. Later, when he saw that she was in trouble in the water, he called the Shore Patrol that brought her in."

11

Dr. Brandon transferred words to paper in a small precise hand before looking up. "Then it bothered you," he said, "this boy living in the same house with you?"

Without will, she nodded.

"Did Leo Cole ever hurt you?"

"He . . . he tried to kiss me. I didn't want him to."

"Anything else?"

". . . things he wanted to do, if I went out with him." As she looked over her shoulder, it seemed as if she could see Leo Cole standing there, his too long hair falling down over his bold, agate-colored eyes. She covered her face with her hands and cried soundlessly.

Dr. Brandon closed the manila folder with a small, contained smile. "I think we've talked enough for one day," he said. He nodded his head in the direction of Miss Marple. "You can take Christina back to the ward and bring the next patient in." He sighed as he glanced down at the newly opened folder that Dr. Zabrowsky handed him.

The girl got to her feet, allowed Miss Marple to guide her from the room.

"There now," Miss Marple said when they were back in the corridor. "That wasn't so bad, was it? And look, I've brought you a ribbon for your hair." She produced it from a starched pocket. "And a brownie I snitched from the kitchen."

The girl took them both, then threw herself face down on the narrow hospital bed.

The windows were small and set close to the ceiling so that the moonlight as it entered the ward seemed less like moonlight than stage lighting for a half-remembered play. When its pale fingers reached the bed in the corner where she lay, Christina sat up. She had not slept, although it seemed hours had passed since Miss King, the nurse on night duty, had come popping into the room and handed her a blue and white sleeping pill in a paper cup and with hearty cheeriness turned off the light.

Not sleeping had been her trouble *that* other night—though how long ago that other night was, she no longer could be sure. Time, like the moonlight, had become unreal. That other night she had lain awake in the small, hot room—as she had every night since her father's funeral—remembering, putting together, arranging, rearranging the pieces of her shattered life only to have them scramble themselves into a new and more frightful picture than the one before.

It was then, in fright and desperation that she had stumbled from her bed; whimpering and groping, she padded in the darkness down the long unfamiliar hall, walking faster, her heart pounding, past the room where Leo Cole slept, to her aunt's bedroom at the rear of the house.

She had tapped lightly at the door, then more loudly. In whispered panic, she had called her name. "Aunt Henriette! Aunt Henriette, *please*."

Aunt Henriette slept soundly and no answer came. The doorknob turned greasily in her hand. Hinges creaked and she stepped into the room. The air was stale, hot, and overlaid with faint medicinal smells. It was, however, less dark here than in the hall. The pale glimmer of light from some source outside the window revealed a large mounded form beneath the sheet. The luminous face of an alarm clock cast a greenish glow on the face on the pillow.

She leaned over, meaning only to touch the mounded shoulder, but in her terror clutched it. "Aunt Henriette, wake up! Help me, help me, please!"

The light went on. Pinpointed in its glare, paralyzed with fright, she sank to her knees by the bed, burying her face in the rumpled sheet as Aunt Henriette had said coolly—"I am helping you, by giving you a home. You're scarcely an heiress, you know—though that's no fault of yours. Your father, like all the rest of the Fredericksons, was longer on fine manners than he was on making money—or, for that matter, hanging on to what he had. Sitting around with his nose in a book while his business

13

went down the drain." Aunt Henriette sniffed dryly, in a way she had. "If I hadn't married Alfred Zengler after your Uncle Leonard died, we'd neither of us have a roof over our heads, and as it is I have to work in an office all day." She shifted her bulk in bed and continued in a voice not unkind. "You've had a difficult time. But nothing is to be gained by hysterics. Run along to bed now, like a good girl. Things will look brighter in the morning."

Dry-eyed, head still bowed, she had scrambled awkwardly to her feet and with a mumbled apology managed to reach the door before the light was extinguished. In darkness that now, by contrast, seemed even more impenetrable than before, she felt her way back to the room Aunt Henriette had given her when her father had brought her there to live a month before. She turned on the light, a single unfrosted bulb inserted in a bracket on the wall, and looked about her. But she did not see the rumpled bed, the chest of drawers blackened with layers of ancient paint, or the scarred mirror above it. She saw their house on Nightingale Hill, remembered the April they'd moved in. How she had laughed as her father scooped up her mother and danced her over the doorsill as easily as, a minute later, he had picked up her skinny fourteen-year-old self!

After that, happy happenings—boy-girl parties, sliding parties, skating parties—had formed an endless chain. She'd made the synchronized swimming team. Gary Schofield had started coming around, then Tim Morton. And best of all—better than boys, who could be a nuisance —her father had taught her to drive. Each day he had come home early from the factory and with him in the seat beside her, her long hair flying, they followed spring down one country road after another.

And then the music stopped.

She'd had no presentiment. She'd come home from school one day during lunch period—Gary had driven her—to get a paper she'd forgotten, and found her father

14

there. Even when he said her mother wasn't feeling well, she had been too wrapped up in her own gay affairs to be alarmed. Her mother had had headaches as long as she could remember. But always the next morning the sun was shining and she was well again.

But not this time. The music had stopped and would never play again. Still, for a while, the carousel went round and round in its strangely silent way as it once had done on a real carousel when she was five or six. Mounted on a gay and prancing steed, she had not missed the music until a man in coveralls, who'd been working at its core, said, "Sorry, folks. That's all."

And that was the way it happened. A week after that May day when Gary brought her home, her mother was dead—dying as simply and as unexpectedly as a light burning out. When school closed, they had moved from Nightingale Hill to a smaller house and at the same time her father's company which, it seemed, hadn't manufactured much of anything for years, closed its doors. Then they'd come here. She to stay with Aunt Henriette until her father, as he said, was on his feet again.

If she had endured a little longer . . . if she had kept the unhappiness from her voice the last time her father called, he would now be alive. But she had not endured. "Hurry, home," she'd whimpered. "I don't like it here. Aunt Henriette is gone all day . . . and there's this boy who hangs around . . ."

"Sit tight, Christy girl," he said. "A traveling job is not the only way to earn a living. I'm on my way. Right now."

Not a dozen hours passed before the Western Union messenger was standing at the door.

"Through my fault, through my fault, through my most grievous fault." The words, spoken half aloud, rose from the recessed memory of a Mass she'd once attended with a Catholic friend. *She knew.* If he had not been tired and worried, if he had not driven all night to reach her sooner, the fatal crash would not have come.

That night after Aunt Henriette had sent her away uncomforted she had moved from the doorway where she had stood immobile as the minutes passed, to the mirror. The girl inside—a girl she did not know—stared back at her. Quickly she turned from the mirror and began to dress, rummaging in the bureau drawer for her clean panties, brassiere, and her best slip. The dress had been new that spring—the last one her mother had ever made for her. Now, like all her clothes, it was too large.

She had not looked at herself again after she was dressed, but turned off the light and descended the stairs in the silent darkness. It was cooler outside, and she drew a deep breath. Feeling calm, peaceful, almost happy, she began walking quickly in the direction of the lake. Then memory stopped as darkness deep and quiet as the lake flowed over her.

She was in the hospital when she next awoke and still there was nothing where the water had been.

"Are these pills tranquilizers?" Christina said, looking at the small white capsule in her hand.

"I'm not supposed to discuss your medication with you," Miss Marple said, "but I see no harm in telling you that they are. They help keep you from worrying while we get things straightened out."

"You mean, get *me* straightened out. My pneumonia has been gone for days."

Miss Marple laughed. "Maybe they are to straighten out both you and things. But in any case, take the pill. I want to see it go down the hatch. Right now."

"You don't trust me," Christina said. She made tears come in her eyes.

"I trust you," Miss Marple said, dryly. "But my orders are to watch you take it. O.K.? Then, I want you to get dressed—there's someone waiting to see you. You'll feel better when you are wearing some clothes of your own. Your aunt sent over a suitcase with some of your things."

The caller was waiting in a small sitting room reserved for visitors. "My name is Miss Stevenson," said the caller. "I'm your probation officer."

Christina did not answer, but cast a sharp appraising glance at the tall young woman with the coil of thick dark hair. A probation officer she might be, but in her dark cotton with its white accents she looked more like a model than an officer of the law.

"If you like, you can call me Steve—lots of others do. As we're going to be seeing a good deal of each other for a while, I thought it was time to get acquainted."

Christina allowed herself a small smile. Even with the charming ones, she had learned it was not best to say too much too soon.

Miss Stevenson nodded as if she agreed. "Dr. Brandon has told me you don't want to live with your aunt. I'd agree with your decision. However, nothing is ever quite as simple as it seems. I'm afraid no decision can be made until Judge Rick appoints a guardian for you and arranges a court hearing. Then, if he should decide that a foster home is the best place for you, there'll be another wait until we find the foster parents that we think are just right."

"Can . . . can I stay here, until then?"

Miss Stevenson shook her head. "Dr. Brandon is pleased with your progress. He signed your release from the hospital this morning. You can continue your therapy at the Juvenile Home until Judge Rick arranges your hearing."

"But I don't want to go there!" Christina cried. "I mean, I can't! I won't!"

"Children in trouble," said Miss Stevenson, "have to have some place to go."

CHAPTER TWO

A Far Cry

Immersed in her own unhappy thoughts since they'd left the hospital, Christina looked up with a new uneasiness as the black Plymouth turned in between the cement pillars.

The dull, red brick building rose at the end of the long straight drive, big, square, and ugly, set in a sea of nothing. Neither tree nor shrub nor wild flower broke the flat expanse of weeds and coarse grass that formed its setting. The whole scene, indeed, might have been the conjuring of an evil witch or a magician.

An impulse to break and run from the car crossed Christina's mind and was as quickly gone. Run where? And to whom? There were no houses. She had not even noticed when the residential district had been left behind. And if she did run, the heavy-set, red-faced man at the wheel of the car would soon overtake her. As if she were a criminal. She had wondered vaguely when they left the hospital why Miss Stevenson had not been driving. Now, she thought, she knew.

When the car stopped, Miss Stevenson got out, holding

her hand for Christina as gaily as if they had been alighting in front of a fine hotel.

"My suitcase," she said, trying hard to make the hotel illusion real.

"Oh, Joe will take that around to the storeroom," Miss Stevenson said. She walked briskly on, not seeming to notice that Christina was lagging one step behind.

As they neared the building, the door opened without a touch of hands, and once inside it closed behind them with a click.

A woman dressed in white looked up from her desk.

"Well, here we are," Miss Stevenson said, as cheerily as at a tea. "Mrs. Moreland, this is Christina Frederickson. Christina, Mrs. Moreland." She laid a folder on the desk then smiled, giving Christina's hand a little squeeze. "I'll be running along, but I'll be back in a few days to see how you are getting on."

The buzzer buzzed, the door opened, closed, and she was gone.

Christina bowed her head. Without willing or wanting, events were again controlling her. Pressed into this new environment, she felt she had neither strength to accept it nor to fight back.

As if from a great distance, she could hear Mrs. Moreland going on about rules, recreation, meals, and dress. She closed her mind to it until Mrs. Moreland rose. Footsteps approached and to Christina's downcast eyes materialized in the form of a pair of extremely large white shoes above which rose the tallest woman she had ever seen.

"This is Miss Pym, the matron on your wing," said Mrs. Moreland. "You will go along with her for a shower, shampoo, and change of clothes. Then she'll take you to your room. You'll not start to school until tomorrow."

"School in summer," Christina thought vaguely. But it did not seem strange. Once again she was a tiny particle caught in a vortex. Spinning round and round, faster and faster, she followed the large white shoes down a long antiseptic hall.

"Shower room and dressing rooms are here," said Miss Pym in a voice that was gruff but not unkind. "I'll wait here until you're through. And while you're about it, shampoo that hair."

"I shampooed it yesterday," said Christina, speaking almost as a reflex.

"Rule," said Miss Pym. "Wash it. And I'll see what I can scare up for you in the way of clothes. No bigger'n a minute, are you? One of my legs is bigger around than your waist." Her large hands moved deftly among piles of panties and brassieres on a long open shelf, then began riffling through a wardrobeful of cotton dresses.

"My own clothes are in my suitcase, but I don't know where it is. . . ."

"Storeroom," said Miss Pym speaking briefly, as if too much conversation might sap her strength. "You'll get it when you leave. Also your dress and other things that you've got on. Now into the shower with you." She looked at a small watch on her massive wrist. "Ten minutes, all told, not a second more."

In the shower stall, eyes closed and with her face uplifted, Christina let the water pour over her. She did not think at all until Miss Pym, in the voice of a football referee, called "Time!" Silently, Christina accepted the towel that was handed her through the curtain, then the pair of cotton panties and bra.

"Now that you've something on, we'll have a go at drying that hair or you'll be sleeping with it wet. And here's a half slip and a dress that I think will fit O.K."

Miss Pym's hands toweling her hair were, for all their size, gentle. The dress, a blue and white print shift, was starched and almost new. Christina put it on mechanically.

"Have a look at yourself in the mirror," Miss Pym said, pleased.

Christina looked, but this time the girl inside was hidden. The outer shell, a thin, fine-boned girl with dark-lashed blue eyes and long straight hair the color of ocean sand, stared back at her. A girl who, when Miss Pym said, "This way," followed; stopped when Miss Pym stopped.

"Here's your room," said Miss Pym, giving the door a little kick with a large white shoe. "Remember, it's the second one beyond the drinking fountain on the right-hand side. I tell you that because the rooms are so much alike. In fact, if you forget the color of your toothbrush you're apt to find yourself sleeping in someone else's bed." With a little snort of laughter at her joke, Miss Pym turned to go. "I'm going to leave you for a while to get your bearings. And if you feel like crying, cry. Most do—for a while."

"Hey! My name's Mitzi. What's yours?"

Although the voice from the doorway was young, chipper, and friendly, Christina lying face to the wall did not move.

"Well, don't answer if you don't want to." The voice as it moved into the room did not seem at all perturbed. "The first time I was here, I didn't speak to anybody for three days. The thing was, nobody could have cared less. Now, they wish I'd shut up. That's why I'm here now—because I was talking in class. 'Creating a disturbance,' Mr. Inrode said. He didn't know I was talking on purpose so he'd send me to my room. I had a good notion you were here."

The giggle that followed was so contagious that Christina turned from one side to the other and between her spread fingers peered at the girl facing her from the cot across the room. Dark eyes, set in a small, clever face framed with a cap of brick-red hair that looked as if its owner might have cut it with a dull knife, returned her curious gaze. Then both girls smiled. Christina shyly. The other with such broad approval that the bedsprings squeaked. "Hey! That's more like it! Maybe I'd better go out and come in all over again."

Christina shook her head.

"Maybe I'd better, anyway." Mischief shone from the girl's dark eyes. "I said my name was Mitzi. But it isn't, really. It's Eva. Did you ever hear anything so ick? *Evva*. Only someone who had it in for a little defenseless baby would name it that. So I changed it to Mitzi. But hardly anyone remembers, except The Pym. She tries."

"I'll call you Mitzi, if you want. My name is Christina."

Mitzi tipped her head like a terrier listening to an unfamiliar sound. "Christina. It's pretty. But what you look like is an Elaine. With all that blond hair, I mean. Elaine—you know—in Tennyson. *The Idylls of the King*." She closed her eyes, folded her hands across her chest and took on, quite suddenly, an air of winsomeness and grace as she recited.

"Elaine, the fair, Elaine, the lovable
Elaine, the lily maid of Astolat,
High in her·chamber, up a tower to the East,
Guarded the sacred shield of Lancelot."

"Why . . . why, thank you." Christina felt tears well in her eyes. "It . . . it's been so long since anyone gave me a compliment."

Mitzi turned away with a shrug. "Oh, that's all right." Her voice was brusque. "It just came into my mind. I guess what I was thinking is that you don't look like a delinquent."

"I'm not," Christina said, stiffly.

"If you haven't done something you shouldn't have, you wouldn't be here," Mitzi said with a careless air. "The dependent kids are kept at Shelter House on the other side of town. They're not locked up."

Christina walked woodenly to the half-opened window at the end of the room and pulled aside the strips of curtain. The heavy wire screening outside the window was too heavy to yield to nail file or knife. The fence around the enclosure at which she looked was too high for climbing. The front door by which she had entered the building a few hours before had closed with an ominous click. She turned away. Though Miss Stevenson hadn't said so, in her heart she had known she would be coming to a place like this.

"Don't let it bug you," Mitzi said. Once again, her tone was cheerful. "There are ways of getting out if you try. The thing is, who wants to? Not me, and that's for sure." She grinned. "I ran away from the foster home they sent me to, knowing I'd get caught and brought back here."

"Nobody would do a thing like that."

"Well, I did. Ask The Pym. I'm pretty sure she knows. And I think Mrs. Moreland is beginning to suspect that is the reason for the trouble I cause. The worse your record here, the harder it is for them to place you in a foster home."

"But your own home. Could . . . couldn't you go back there?"

"Not on your life! Even if my mother'd have me—which she's not about to do. She didn't want me when I was born and I've not become any more desirable as time goes by. As for my father, where he is and what he's doing I haven't the faintest. The thing is, I like it here." Her dark eyes sought Christina's for understanding. "Maybe, when you've been here longer you'll see how it is. You don't expect anything of anybody, and they don't expect anything of you. That way, nobody's disappointed. Best of all, you don't have to *love* anybody. Do you . . . do you see what I mean?!"

Puzzled, Christina shook her head. "I'm not sure."

"Well, don't lose any sleep over it," Mitzi said, her sanguine self again. "Even if you don't have to love anybody it's nice to have a friend."

When Christina awoke, a small white ghost was leaning over her. It turned into Mitzi as it spoke.

"Hey, kid. Wake up. You were dreaming. You said something queer. You said, 'The music stopped,' then you began to cry."

"I . . . I know." Though the room was heavy with the heat of late August, Christina shivered in her thin print gown. "I . . . dream sometimes."

Mitzi had gone back to her bed, vanishing in the deep shadows. "Sometimes, telling helps. I mean, if you want to."

"I've forgotten it already," Christina said, too quickly, then added, "You know how dreams are," hoping to make amends.

"Yeah, I know." Mitzi yawned to show she didn't care.

Christina turned to the wall, lying stiff and still in the darkness. Even if Mitzi's feelings were hurt, she could not talk about the dream and all that happened after without revealing the guilt that weighed so heavily on her heart. And if she told, could Mitzi understand?

Nor was that the only question. How was it that Mitzi, deprived and rejected from the day she was born, had developed a tough protective covering that inured her to love while she herself had not wanted to live when love was gone?

"Don't let it bug you," Mitzi said from across the way, as accurately as if she'd read Christina's mind, which perhaps she had.

Christina smiled, then turned on her stomach and thinking about Mitzi, not herself, fell asleep as peacefully as she used to do in the house on Nightingale Hill.

CHAPTER THREE

Ward of the Court

"A 'guardian ad litem,'" Mitzi wrote, crinkling her nose. "What's that?"

Christina took the paper, half a sheet torn from a notebook, that Mitzi passed across the aisle and beneath her friend's scrawl printed, "It's a man—a lawyer, I guess—that the judge appointed to see that my legal rights are preserved."

The paper was barely back in Mitzi's possession before Mr. Inrode, tall, thin, and stooped, looking rather like a latter-day Ichabod Crane, looked up from his desk and said dryly, "I daresay that the information you and Christina have been so busily passing back and forth across the aisle is of such vital importance that it would not keep until after class?"

"Well, it *is* pretty important, Mr. Inrode," Mitzi said, her face as guileless as a baby's. "For Christina, anyway. Coming into class today she told me that Miss Stevenson told her that Judge Rick had appointed a 'guardian ad litem' for her. Christina didn't have time to explain what that meant, so I wrote a note and asked her—and she wrote back to tell me. But I really should have known that 'litem' is the Latin accusative of lis-litis—in general, a strife, dispute, quarrel, or altercation, especially in law—a suit, action, litigation, or controversy." Mitzi shut her eyes in concentration. "It's all coming back."

"That's enough," said Mr. Inrode, taking a deep breath for strength. "*I* know what it means. But I doubt if anyone else in the room is interested. Now get busy and finish your assignment."

"I've finished my assignment, Mr. Inrode," Mitzi said meekly. "And everyone *is* interested. Just look."

It could not be disputed. All work in the room had stopped. Sixteen pairs of eyes had turned from Mitzi to Christina and back to Mitzi again.

"Mitzi!" Mr. Inrode's patience, a frail vessel at best, had shattered under the strain.

"I'm sorry, Mr. Inrode," Mitzi said. "I'll try to find something to keep me busy." Although she had assumed a chastened tone the look she gave Christina was triumphant.

Embarrassedly, Christina bent over her own assignment. Poor Mr. Inrode! How could he hope to teach a conglomeration of students whose intelligence ranged from low (Bennie Dorgan, ninth grade) to high (who else but Mitzi, a senior)? Yet, in a quiet time like this that always followed an upheaval—the only sound was that of the clock ticking loudly on Mr. Inrode's desk—this might have been a schoolroom anywhere.

If Mitzi, who seemed to have private pipelines of information, had not told her, she would never have known that Joey, the frail-looking boy with the face of an elderly man who sat directly in line with Mr. Inrode's all-seeing eye, had shot and seriously wounded his drunken father. Or that Grace, a large girl with a soft voice and manners, was waiting trial for shoplifting. She'd stolen clothing, Mitzi said. Nothing for herself, but for a younger sister she adored.

Strangely enough, Christina thought dreamily as her mind floated away from the book before her, the problem of each person in the room was like an iceberg. The largest part, the hazardous part, was concealed below the surface. Dangerous water in which to travel. And what would *she* have done, how would *she* have fared without Mitzi who, like a small armored tugboat, piloted her successfully through each day? In the dining room, in the small library where the girls were herded together before classes or bells rang for meals, in the recreation room after dinner when, for an hour or two, girls and boys were together, Mitzi was always nearby, alert and pugnacious.

Once, when a tall, withdrawn boy, who seldom talked at all had sidled up to her to ask "What are you in here for?" Mitzi had pushed her way between them, her lower jaw out-thrust. "In for?" she had countered. "What do you mean 'in for'? She's here, that's all. What business is it of yours anyway?"

Afterward, when she and Mitzi were alone, Mitzi'd said, "He's a nut. Don't pay any attention to him." That was all she'd say, and Christina shut it from her mind. With the help of the pills she got twice daily from the nurse, who watched her just as closely as Miss Marple had, all that had happened before no longer had such dreadful focus in her thoughts. She had even learned to parry the questions of Dr. Wheat, a young man as colorless as his name who wasn't a real doctor at all (according to Mitzi) but a psychologist who came to the Home twice a week and who was bent on prying into her past.

Until Miss Stevenson had told her that morning that a guardian had been appointed for her, she had been so inclosed in the ordered, austere life of the home that she had almost forgotten that on the "outside" plans were being made for her future.

"Don't worry," Miss Stevenson had said with her usual cheerfulness. "He'll be out to see you before the hearing, to get acquainted." There had been more Miss Stevenson said, but she hadn't listened. As she wasn't listening now.

"Christina," Mr. Inrode was saying. "*Christina.* Will you pay attention, please?"

Christina looked up, suddenly aware of the large white shape of Miss Pym, standing like an enormous angel at her side.

"Mrs. Moreland wants you in the office. You're to come with me," Miss Pym said in a whisper that could be heard around the room.

Flushing, Christina got to her feet.

"What a goof ball," someone said, and laughed.

"Silence!" said Mr. Inrode, in an unaccustomed roar.

Her heart pounding, Christina followed Miss Pym's broad back from the room.

"Just someone to see you, that's all," said Miss Pym reassuringly, when they were outside the room. "No need to be afraid."

"Not a boy—nor a woman? Someone rather . . . (she almost said 'large') fat?"

"Bless you, no," said Miss Pym. She tapped at the open door of Mrs. Moreland's glass-walled office. The man turned, rose slowly from the chair. Tall. Taller than Miss Pym. Much. He looked, thought Christina with a little start, as Abraham Lincoln must have looked as a young man when he was a lawyer in Illinois.

He moved toward her with an awkward yet easy grace, a strong, long-fingered hand outstretched.

"I'm Dave Keller," he said. His voice had the pleasant rumbly quality her father's voice had had. She felt the smart of tears and turned her head.

"Will you take Mr. Keller and Christina to Conference Room B?" Mrs. Moreland said. She smiled a little as the tall, dark-haired man ducked his head as he passed through the doorway and followed Miss Pym down the hall.

Christina walked beside him blindly. Had he reached

for her hand and held it, as one does the hand of a trusting child, she would not have pulled it away.

The small, neatly furnished room was the same one in which Miss Pym had left her earlier in the day when she had her conference with Miss Stevenson.

Dave Keller took a rumpled package of cigarettes from the pocket of his suit, looked at it ruefully and put it back. "Cutting down," he said. "A preliminary to cutting them out entirely, as the doctor says I'd better do if I want to live to a ripe old age. You smoke?" he added, though he made no move to offer her the rumpled pack.

Christina shook her head. "I . . . my father said . . ."

"What did he say? I'm interested."

"He said . . . that if a girl smoked, before long her hair and her breath and all her clothes smelled like stale tobacco. It sounded so awful that, well, I didn't want to try."

Dave Keller grinned. "Pretty smart dad. Smart girl, too. I'm glad my wife doesn't smoke. And my son is too young. Only six. Though I did read in the paper the other night that forty percent of the kids in some eastern grade school were smoking cigarettes by the age of eight."

"Where do such little kids get the money?" She had asked the question with such honest astonishment that Dave Keller threw back his head and laughed.

Then Christina laughed so spontaneously that Miss Pym passing by nodded as approvingly as if she had elicited it herself.

"We'll get along," Dave Keller said, still smiling. "When Judge Rick asked me to take this guardianship, I almost said 'no.' Not for any reason that concerns you. I just happen to be involved with a number of other things." He got to his feet, once again extended a long lean hand. "Your hearing is set for tomorrow morning. When Judge Rick called to tell me it was coming up tomorrow I decided I'd better get myself out here so we could get acquainted."

31

"Tomorrow?" Christina faltered. "I . . . I didn't think it would be so soon."

"You've been here long enough," Dave Keller said a little grimly. "Even so, unless the judge thinks it is best for you to live with your aunt, in which case you would immediately go home with her, it will be necessary for you to return here until a suitable foster home can be found."

"I'd die before I went back to my aunt's. . . ." The words were spoken and their significance mirrored on Dave Keller's face before she realized what she had said.

"You won't go back to your aunt's house if I can help it. I visited your aunt this morning. I would not recommend your returning there." A muscle tightened along the line of his jaw. "The court may have appointed me to protect only your legal rights, but a lawyer's job is a little more than that. The rights of the individual must be protected, too." He grinned. "Well, here I am—up on my soapbox again. No wonder my wife wishes I'd joined her father's law firm. They do probate and corporate work only. But I'm not going to burden you with that. Miss Stevenson will pick you up tomorrow morning about eight-thirty. Wear a pretty dress—and put a ribbon in your hair."

Like a giant genie, Miss Pym appeared as Dave Keller and Christina stepped into the hall. "Until tomorrow," he said. He bowed gravely, every inch an attorney-at-law.

"Until tomorrow," said Christina.

Miss Pym did not say "come along," until the tall, loosely-put-together figure had turned the corner and was out of sight.

Inside the Courthouse pedestrian traffic was heavier than on the street outside. Heels clicked, shuffled, or trod briskly on the mottled marble floor. Children cried as they were hauled along on parents' errands. A black and white mongrel dog, trotting as briskly along as if on business of his own, stopped in front of the elevator where, with a half-dozen other people, Miss Stevenson and Christina waited.

When the people had all got on the elevator, the operator—a small, rotund man with a tonsure of white hair—addressed the dog. "Please take the elevator on the other side of the lobby. The dog licensing division is on the third floor at the end of the corridor."

Everyone laughed except Christina, who had not heard. All the confidence that Dave Keller had inspired in her the day before had vanished by the time the front door of the Home had closed behind him. Mitzi had done her best—exhorting, assuring, finally becoming vehement. "Even if the judge says you have to go back to your Aunt Henriette's it's not the end of the world. You can move out for good as soon as you're eighteen. Then you'll be on your own. In the meantime, tell that Leo person that if he as much as touches you, you'll scream. Better yet, tell him that you'll tell your guardian—after all, he ought to be good for something—and that he will take your story to the judge."

But nothing that Mitzi could say had reassured her. By the time Miss Stevenson had picked her up in the black Plymouth that morning—this time, they were alone—her future looked as bleak as it had the midnight she had stood alone in the back bedroom at Aunt Henriette's.

"Judge Rick's chambers are this way," Miss Stevenson said brightly, when the elevator stopped to let them out. She took Christina's arm and propelled her the length of another marble hall. Here, the only other person in sight was a janitor polishing the brass railing that overlooked the lobby three floors below. Muffled, shuffling noises floated up, forming the background for the staccato clip of Miss Stevenson's trim, patent pumps. Christina's flats made no sound at all.

The door before which they stopped was ornately carved, but the sign above it simply said "Judge Rick."

"We're here right on the dot," Miss Stevenson said,

looking at her watch. "I expect the others are already here."

Afterward the large windowless room with its dark paneled walls, the furnishings, the people in it, were to remain in Christina's mind with the clarity of a tableau. At one end stood the judge's bench—vacant now, but so formidable a fortress and so high that it could only be approached on either side by steps. At the other end were the jurors' chairs, carved of the same dark wood. A calendar, depicting a happy hunter and his dog, hung from a nail on the mustard-colored plastering above the wainscot. A large American flag rested in a standard on the floor. At the conference-type table sat Aunt Henriette and Dave Keller.

Christina stood so still that not until a long minute or two had passed, did she feel Miss Stevenson gently nudging her and whispering, "Go on in."

Aunt Henriette rose. Large, imposing, dressed in black, she moved majestically toward Christina. "My poor child," she whispered. "My poor little girl."

Christina stiffened under the strong fat fingers gripping her arm. A moment later, Dave Keller was towering over them both. "You'd best sit down, Mrs. Zengler." His voice was so firm, yet kindly, that Aunt Henriette, surprised, allowed herself to be lowered into her chair. "And you, Christina," he added, "can sit here by me."

The minute hand of the clock on the wall jumped noisily. Christina could feel her heart move with it as an inside door at the end of the courtroom opened and a slight man with thinning, pinkish hair came through. He sat down without speaking at the far end of the table and settled the small black box he had been carrying before him.

"Court reporter," Dave Keller said. "That box is called a stenotype. He can take dictation on it faster than you can talk. Two hundred and twenty words a minute, possibly more." He paused, pushed back his chair, and whispered to Christina, "Stand up. Here comes the judge now."

If Dave Keller had not identified the pleasant-looking man with the bright blue eyes as the judge, Christina would not have known. For he was not dressed in long, flowing black robes as she had imagined he would be, nor did he ascend the steps to the bench. Instead, he walked toward the table from which all the others had now risen.

"Judge Rick, may I present Christina Frederickson?" It was Miss Stevenson speaking, formally and smoothly.

"Christina." Judge Rick's repsonse was grave.

"And Christina's aunt—her father's sister-in-law, Mrs. Zengler."

"Mrs. Zengler."

"And, of course, you know Mr. Keller."

"I do." The judge smiled slightly and sat down.

"If it pleases your Honor, then, we will begin," Miss Stevenson said. She opened the folder before her, glanced at it briefly, then at the slight man with the pinkish hair whose fingers had started playing over the surface of the black box as soon as she started to speak. "The purpose of requesting this hearing is, as you know, to determine what best possible arrangement can be made for the future welfare of Christina Marianne Frederickson who, as the result of losing both parents, and having no close blood relatives, has been made and is now a ward of the court. As such, she has been placed in the custody of the Maple County Children's Home Society."

"And your recommendation, Miss Stevenson?"

"My recommendation, your Honor, is that Christina be placed in a foster home as soon as one deemed suitable can be found. I have reached this opinion as the result of conferences with Dr. Brandon at City Hospital, Miss Few of the Child Welfare office, Mr. Keller, and Christina, herself."

"Mr. Keller, as Christina's guardian may I also have your opinion, please?"

"I am in agreement with Miss . . ."

"And what about me?" Aunt Henriette interrupted. A dark flush suffused her face as she leaned forward in her chair, one outspread hand making a sharp slapping sound as it struck the table before her. "Are the wishes of the only person in the room who has a real interest in this child to be ignored?"

Christina, who had drawn into herself as the conversation eddied about her, looked up with a start. Her frightened eyes traveled from her aunt's darkened visage to that of the judge.

"You are speaking extravagantly, Mrs. Zengler," Judge Rick said mildly. "Nevertheless, you are entitled to express your opinion."

"If I may speak then," said Aunt Henriette tartly, "I would like to point out that Christina's father would scarcely have brought her to me in the first place if he had not thought me a suitable person to look after her in his absence, or if he had not thought my home a proper place for a young girl to live. Christina's . . . er . . . unfortunate experience is scarcely one that *I* can be held responsible for."

"Mrs. Zengler, please," Miss Stevenson interposed quickly and soothingly. "No one is criticizing you or your home. My recommendation is based only on what I feel are Christina's particular needs at this rather trying time."

"Her *particular* needs, your Honor, are some discipline and responsibility," Aunt Henriette said dryly. "And I think I would be derelict in my duty to my dead husband, who was fond of Christina as a young child, if I turned her over to strangers when I have the strength and desire to provide for her. I have been in touch this past week with her father's lawyer in Spring Valley and he informs me that, fortunately, Christina will inherit a little money. Not much, but enough that if carefully invested it will give her a small monthly allowance and see her through college."

As Aunt Henriette talked, her voice turned creamy, her

smile benign. "Most importantly, Judge Rick, I can take Christina home with me today. Surely, this would be a better course than to send the child back to the Home—scarcely a good environment for a delicately brought-up young girl—to stay until a suitable foster home is found for her. For a child like Christina, with her . . . er . . . problems, this might not be easy. I am already making a home for my nephew," she added virtuously, "and one more child . . ."

Dave Keller pushed back his chair with an unpleasant scraping sound. His low-pitched voice was so quietly intense when he spoke that the court reporter who had been sitting impassively with the black box since the hearing began, looked up. "Your Honor," said Dave Keller, "my request is unusual, but could I talk to you outside the courtroom? For a few minutes. Alone?"

"Why, yes. If you wish."

Dave Keller's fingers touched Christina's shoulder with a moment's pressure then followed Judge Rick from the room.

"And just what is the purpose of that maneuver?" Aunt Henriette demanded. "If that Mr. Keller has something to say to the judge, why can't he say it in front of everyone?"

"It is the judge's privilege to grant such a request, if he wishes," Miss Stevenson said. Though she spoke calmly, to Christina this very calmness seemed to increase rather than to detract from the nightmarish quality of the scene in which she, unwillingly, was not only spectator but principal character. The thing that she had convinced herself could not happen, was going to happen. In spite of everything that Dave Keller might say, the judge would decree that she must return home with Aunt Henriette. For how could the judge believe other than that her father had brought her to live with Aunt Henriette just because he *did* think her a suitable person? Might not the judge think, too, that if she did not go with Aunt Henriette that no foster parent would want her?

37

When the two men came back into the courtroom, Christina dared not look up. The judge spoke first, as she knew he would do.

"As Mrs. Zengler herself pointed out it would not be advisable for Christina to be kept in the Juvenile Home any longer than necessary. As she also pointed out, a proper foster home might not be soon available. This brings me to the rather unusual situation that has developed here this morning. In fact, in the ten years I have been a judge of the Juvenile Court, I have never had a request such as Mr. Keller made when he asked to speak to me outside the courtroom a few minutes ago. The question, however, is one for Christina to answer, not me."

Through a blur of tears, Christina raised her eyes. The judge was smiling. Miss Stevenson was thrusting a handkerchief into her hand.

"Would you like to live with Mr. and Mrs. Keller?"

For a moment she thought she could not have heard correctly. But if she had mis-heard, why was everybody smiling? The judge, Dave Keller, Miss Stevenson, even the man with the little black box. Everybody but Aunt Henriette.

She could not speak, only bob her head up and down and then like a booby burst into tears.

"Then that's settled." Now the judge was smiling broadly. "And I think settled very well. Floradale is a nice community. It has an excellent high school. One small boy for Christina to help look after should not interfere too much with her activities. I think all that is necessary now, is to sign a release so she can leave the Home. Then anytime you and Mrs. Keller are ready to pick her up, there'll be no delay."

Aunt Henriette, stiff with displeasure, pushed back her chair. "A parody of justice," she huffed. "The matter will not rest here."

"The matter will rest here," Judge Rick said quietly. "In fact, if I did not think you sincere in your desire to give Christina a home, I would cite you for contempt of court. And I shall still do so if any more such remarks are forthcoming. Now, if I may return to what I was saying . . . I will sign Christina's release from the Home so anytime you are ready to pick her up there will be no delay."

"We will be ready, your Honor, today. I'll call Mrs. Keller and tell her the good news immediately, then drive out and pick Christina up when I leave my office about five this afternoon."

Judge Rick nodded approval. "Oh, yes. One more thing. Christina should continue with therapy until she is completely well again. Whom she should see, however, I'll leave to your and Miss Stevenson's good judgment." The gavel hit the table with a thud. Judge Rick said, "This hearing is adjourned."

CHAPTER FOUR

The House on Peony Place

"I'm leaving," Christina said, "in just a little bit." The attempt to keep her voice firm failed miserably as she added, "Mr. Keller is coming to pick me up around five. Aren't . . . aren't you going to say good-bye?"

With a jerk, Mitzi averted her head and with shoulders hunched walked toward the window.

Christina took a step toward her but stopped as Mitzi swung around to face her with a harsh little laugh. "Good-bye? Of course, I'll say 'good-bye.' Why not? Here today and gone tomorrow, that's my motto. Who knows what tomorrow may bring? Tomorrow—in spite of everything I say—somebody may want *me*. Preferably," she added, as she struck a pose, "a rich old lady. Although she is embittered by the loss of her child, a beautiful girl with gorgeous blue teeth and curly white eyes, I shall win her over with my ever-loving ways. When she dies, she'll leave me a million dollars in cash and I'll live happily ever after."

Christina put her hands to her eyes, knuckling at the tears. "Don't," she wailed.

"Don't you," Mitzi said fiercely. "Don't you *dare* to cry! Do you think I could manage a minute if I let *myself* cry? Could I survive if I let *myself* care?"

She thrust a wad of tissue into Christina's hand. "Wipe your eyes and straighten up. You don't want your marvelous Mr. Keller to see you've been crying. Or more important, *Mrs.* Keller. Women for all of being known as the softer sex, aren't much on tears. Other people's, I mean."

Christina wiped at her eyes. "I . . . I don't want to cry."

"If you'd stop examining all of your feelings under a microscope you wouldn't feel so sorry for yourself," Mitzi said, still fiercely. "We'll see each other some time or other. Maybe."

"Mr. Keller gave me his address. I wrote it down for you."

Mitzi took the twice folded piece of note paper that Christina gave her, opened it, then tossed it on the bed. "Peony Place. A pretty fancy address, if you ask me. Isn't that out in Floradale?"

"It's in Floradale, but I don't think Mr. Keller's 'fancy,' as you say. Just nice."

"Well, you'll soon find out," Mitzi retorted. "Here's The Pym come to fetch you now."

The small suitcase that Christina had brought with her when she came to the Home looked like a toy dangling from Miss Pym's large hand.

"Though it's four weeks to the day, it doesn't seem like any time at all since I brought you in here and left you to the tender mercies of that one," Miss Pym said, with a jerk of her head toward Mitzi but tempering the remark with a grin. "And I must say," she added approvingly, "you look nice with that ribbon in your hair."

Christina touched her hand to the blue silk band—the same ribbon that Miss Marple had given her in the hospital. How kind Miss Marple had been to her . . . how kind Mitzi and Miss Pym. She bit hard into her lip.

Miss Pym said, "Come along."

Christina said, "Good-bye," but Mitzi did not answer. Already she had walked away and was standing ramrod straight looking out of the window that led to nowhere.

"Her name is Portia," Dave Keller said. He gave the hood of the old green car a pat before opening the door for Christina. "I'd say she is just about your age, though you look a good deal younger. I made the down payment on her with the first fee I collected after I became a lawyer. I say 'collected' because, for almost a year, I handled cases for clients who had one thing in common. No money. But it was good experience. And it made me appreciate Portia all the more when I did get her—though my wife says now that she is a shame and a disgrace."

Christina gave Dave Keller a small grateful smile. "I think she's awfully nice."

"You drive?"

"I did. In Spring Valley. My . . . father taught me. I got my license just before my mother died."

"One of these days I'll let you have a go at Portia," Dave Keller said. "Unfortunately, most of the time it's a case of whither I go, Portia goeth also. I leave the VW, which around our house is referred to as 'the good car,' for my wife to use."

Again Christina smiled, accompanying it with an unintelligible little murmur. It was the best she could do to show her gratitude for the effort he was making to put her at her ease. Then, little by little, as the miles spun out beneath the wheels of the old car, she felt the tension within her begin to ease. Sometimes Dave Keller talked. When he did not, neither his silence nor hers seemed uncompanionable.

"The completion of the freeway has cut my getting-home time in half," Dave Keller said, as he escaped from one of the city's busiest streets onto a descending arc from which a divided four-lane highway stretched westward. At the very end, a great orange sun seemed to hang like a medallion.

"I don't know where I am," Christina said mostly to herself. In spite of her disorientation she did not feel afraid. Traveling on this golden highway Aunt Henriette's house on Slinker Street—even Aunt Henriette herself—might never have existed.

"The lake gets people confused about directions," Dave Keller said, "because it's shaped like a large half moon. For example, your Aunt Henriette's house, which lies east of here, is not far from the lake. While Floradale, which is west of where we are now, is also on the lake. I'll show you a map of the city when we get home so you can get the picture."

Christina breathed deeply, the way she had taught herself to do. It helped slow the beating of her heart. The sun no longer hung by its invisible cord at the end of the highway but seemed to have moved to the right, engulfing the sky with crimson light. A sign above the freeway said, "Floradale Exit 1/2 Mile."

"At one time Floradale was in the country," Dave Keller said. "In fact, when my grandfather built the house we live in now, it was *in* the country. Although he worked in the city—he was a lawyer, too—he didn't want his children brought up there. He had his wish for a while, but by the time my father started to college the city was encroaching. This is what our part of the country looks like now."

As he spoke, Dave Keller swung the green car down the exit from the freeway onto a suburban street much like any other. Heavy with homebound traffic it might have been, Christina thought with a sense of shock, in Spring Valley. The tall man beside her might have been her father. She looked away, only to look again as Dave Keller said, "Here's the high school you'll go to. It's one of the city's biggest. Eighteen hundred students when school started a week ago."

Christina felt new misgiving. The sprawling stone and concrete structure covered half a city block. Eighteen hundred students and she would not know one of them. At George Washington High in Spring Valley there had been less than a thousand. And she'd known everyone in the sophomore class.

"And this is Peony Place. Our street. And this is the house we live in." As the car swung between two pillars flanked by a handsome wrought iron fence and chugged up the shrub-bordered drive, Christina drew in her breath. She had expected an old house, but not one so beautiful. High and handsome, balconied and turreted, its pink brick glowed softly. Its corniced windows winked in the slanting rays of sunlight.

"She's quite an old lady," Dave Keller said, "and not treated the way she deserves. She needs a new roof and her trim painted but maybe someday . . ." He laughed. "But someday, I've also promised my wife a new house. All on one floor. This one, she tells me, is a woman killer. But I'm hoping that you can save her some running with young Dave."

"I'll try," Christina mumbled. "And I want to thank you—for everything."

"You mustn't thank me," Dave Keller said gravely. "I'm afraid I was quite selfish in asking Judge Rick to give us the privilege of being foster parents. We lost a baby before birth. A little girl. She would be eleven now."

"Oh," Christina said, surprised, then added quickly, "I'm sorry."

"It was a bad blow. Particularly, because we had to wait so long before Davey came along. And speaking of Davey, it's easy to see that there's a boy around the house." He pulled the car to a stop, got out and moved a tricycle and a wagon from the driveway, then drove around to the rear of the house where a pink brick carriage house stood, its double doors open. "The VW's gone, she's not home," he said with a puzzled frown. "That means Davey's

45

not here either. Well, they'll be back soon. We can go in the back door, since you are now one of the family."

Christina followed diffidently, pausing just inside the door. The big old-fashioned kitchen in which she stood was spotless; the copper-bottomed pans over the stove were burnished. Her mother had had pans like that, but in *her* kitchen there were the lovely smells of the kind of food she liked—smells of bread baking, soup simmering, spices mingling. Here, on the counter near the sink a package of frozen broccoli was defrosting and there was nothing on the stove at all.

Dave Keller had moved on through the butler's pantry, shelved to the ceiling, into the dining room. "Found a note," he said. He had started to retrace his steps when Christina appeared. "She's gone to pick Davey up at the Printemps'. They've a little boy, Timmy, also in the first grade. Davey frequently goes home after school to play with him. Unfortunately, there aren't any other children on the street anywhere near his age. Natalie . . . my wife encourages it." He looked at his watch. "She and Davey should be back soon, but there's no need for you to wait to get settled."

Christina ran her hand along the satin-smooth railing as Dave Keller preceded her up the stair. A stained-glass window at the halfway point cast a rosy glow into the foyer below. The drawing room that led from it lay in shadows.

In the hall above, Dave Keller was saying, "I thought you might like the tower room better than this, but my wife thought it might put you pretty far away from Davey at night if we happened to be gone."

"This room is very nice."

"If you like old things it's all right," Dave Keller said, smiling. "I try to convince Mrs. Keller that marble bureau tops are coming back in style, but she says that black walnut beds like this one that weigh half a ton, are not. In any case, you'll be comfortable. And when you get some of

46

your own pictures and things out, you'll feel more as if it belongs to you. Now, I'll get your bags out of the car. I think I forgot to tell you that earlier today I stopped by your Aunt Henriette's and picked up your other things."

Christina moved slowly into the room. She walked lightly, as one does in a place where one does not belong, trailing her fingers across the intricately pieced quilt on the bed, feeling the smooth cool marble of the washstand on which stood an old wash bowl and pitcher. All these things, she thought, were probably in the family when Dave Keller's great-grandparents came west a century before.

Then her smile faded as a car door slammed and a child's high happy voice called out, "Daddy! We're home!"

From the window overlooking the back yard she could see a wirey-looking little boy, with a shock of black hair, jump out of a red Volkswagen and hurl himself toward his father.

Dave Keller put down the suitcases he was carrying, held the little boy tightly for a moment, then greeted the slim, handsome woman who turned her face toward him to be kissed. As they started toward the house, Davey broke away from his father's hand and darted back to the car. "Wait!" he cried "Wait for Mr. Hawkins!"

A minute later, Davey rejoined them carrying a large and, even from the distance at which Christina surveyed the scene, scrofulous-looking teddy bear. She turned from the window. How foolish to think, even for a moment, that within this small tightly-knit family—just such a one as she had had—that there would be room for two more. Not just Christina Marianne Frederickson, but for the girl inside.

CHAPTER FIVE

Everyone Knows Everyone

"It's hardly dark enough for candles," Natalie Keller said, "but I think I shall light them anyway, for this is a festive occasion."

Christina mumbled a thank-you. All through the preparation of dinner which Mrs. Keller had gone about briskly and efficiently, she had not only felt helpless but almost as if she were in the way. In fact, she told Christina to sit down saying that she could manage very nicely by herself. Though this seemed more than likely, Christina had propped herself against the refrigerator hoping there'd be something she could do.

The candles lighted, Mrs. Keller held the match for Davey to blow out then said, "You can tell Daddy that dinner is ready."

"Daddy doesn't need to be told, he's here," Dave Keller said. He had changed from his business suit to a pair of khaki wash pants and an old blue shirt. He held the chair for his wife, then Christina; pushed David closer to the table.

Dinner progressed painfully. Christina answered when

spoken to, but no scrap or crumb of conversation could she generate. Even the business of eating required concentration.

The Kellers appeared not to notice, but when David was more than halfway through his own small portion he said in a hoarse whisper, "If you don't eat everything you won't get any dessert."

"David!" His mother spoke in mock reproof. "Christina may have dessert if she wishes—though I'm afraid it won't be any great treat. I've never really mastered pie." She made a little face. "Either my crust is of the imperishable variety no knife can cut, or else it is so tender that it disintegrates at a glance."

"I have a disintegrator!" David cried. His eyes, deep blue and black-lashed like his mother's, were solemn. "It's a ray. I can disintegrate pie. I can disintegrate people! I can . . ."

"David!" said his father. "That's enough."

Grinning, the little boy ducked his head over his plate.

"I'll serve it, if you're ready," Christina said. Already she had her own almost untouched plate in her hand and was ready to push back her chair when Mrs. Keller said, "Thank you, dear, but I do think you had better let me . . ."

"Natalie, please?"

Natalie Keller shrugged lightly, sat back with a little smile.

Cheeks burning, Christina removed the dinner plates and the serving dishes to the kitchen and took up four pieces of lemon pie, mangling them badly in the process. Carrying two pieces, she placed one before Mrs. Keller, the other before her husband. On the second trip, Davey's made it safely to the table but her own plate, as she prepared to put it down, dropped from her hand and landed with a sickening crash on the floor.

There was a moment's hideous silence before anyone

spoke, then Mrs. Keller was out of her chair and had the remains scooped back on one of the pieces of broken plate. "It's all right," she said.

"I'll get a wet cloth." Dave Keller was on the way to the kitchen as he spoke.

Christina stood by helplessly as the plate and pie were removed and the spot on the carpet sponged and patted.

"Good as new," Dave Keller said.

"It will scarcely show," said Natalie Keller.

David watched the proceedings with interest. "If you *meant* to drop it," he advised, "it was naughty. If it was an accident, then you're not. *Did* you mean to?" His tone held hope. Christina shook her head. Tears welled in her eyes.

"There's more pie in the kitchen, if you'd like a piece," Mrs. Keller murmured.

"Thank you, but I . . . I couldn't. May I please be excused?"

"Certainly." Both Kellers spoke at once.

Christina escaped to the kitchen, where she began scraping and rinsing the dishes. The plate she held in her hand was white, fragile, with a delicate raised design and was of the same pattern as the dish she had broken. She turned it over and her heart gave a little lurch of despair as she read the words, "Haviland, France." She should have known. Ever since she could remember, her mother had got out Grandmother Harold's Haviland china for special occasions. White, scattered with forget-me-nots, it had been placed in storage when they had moved out of the house on Nightingale Hill. Someday, if someday ever came, it would be hers—but all the forget-me-not china in the world would not replace the piece of Mrs. Keller's china that she had broken.

As fresh tears began to fall, a line that Mitzi had quoted to her one night when she lay crying in the darkness came back to her. "Here lies one whose name was writ in water," Mitzi had said with an abysmal sigh. "Keats wrote it for his own epitaph, but it might as well be yours. Cry, cry, cry, is all you do."

If Mitzi were here in the kitchen with her now, she knew what Mitzi would say—could almost hear her say it. "You'd feel better if she'd been mean, wouldn't you? Then you could really cry your eyes out. But what happens? She's nice—even when you've broken some stupid plate that probably belonged to her stupid great-grandmother. And what do you do? Bawl."

Christina wiped her eyes on the end of a towel and gave a monumental sniff. Even thinking about Mitzi was good therapy. A little later when Mrs. Keller came out in the kitchen, Christina's nose looked pinched and red but she was not crying. They got through the dishes and an hour of desultory conversation while Dave Keller romped with David but it was still a relief when Mrs. Keller suggested Christina might be tired and want to go to her room.

Upstairs, Mrs. Keller who had followed, pointed out the linen closet where she would find wash cloth and towels and the bathroom at the end of the hall. "Old houses weren't long on bath facilities," she added, "so on this floor we all have to take turns. There's a shower in the basement, though, that you can use if you're in a hurry."

At the door of Christina's room she stopped again. "I hope you'll be comfortable. If there's anything you need or want, let me know. Dave . . . my husband leaves for the office about a quarter after seven. He can drop you at school on his way, though you may not want to leave that early." She smiled a little ruefully. "I wish *he* didn't leave so early," adding as a little afterthought, "he works too hard."

"Tomorrow morning, I'll walk," Christina said. "It will help me to get oriented." She was about to add, "And I can help you get breakfast," but thought better of it.

"Oh, yes, another thing. Sometimes Davey has bad dreams and calls out in his sleep. Don't get up, or be alarmed. I always hear him." Mrs. Keller stood a moment longer as if she, too, had been about to say something more and then changed her mind. "Good night."

"Good night." Christina watched as the white dress flickered down the hall and disappeared into the library where Dave Keller had gone to work on briefs.

Christina shut the door of her room and turning off the light knelt at the open window. "Dear God, please. . . ." She did not go on. The only prayer that came to her lips since her father's death was one that she could neither formulate nor finish. She undressed quickly, brushed her teeth, and slipped between the clean cool sheets, meaning to think about school the next day. *Worry* about school, really. Instead, her mind recreated for her all the incidents of the day beginning with the happenings in the courtroom that morning and ending with the conversation she had had with Mrs. Keller at the door of her room. Except for Aunt Henriette's outburst—now, remembering, she felt a little stir of pity for Aunt Henriette as she had looked, a massive woman-shaped balloon, when she deflated at the judge's sharp threat of contempt—there had been no unpleasantness. Yet, almost always, there had been small tensions, cross currents, invisible involvements at work. All were too tenuous to be described. Some even might be—perhaps were—the products of her imagination. One thing only did she decide. That she would call them Mr. and Mrs. Keller. How they referred to each other when they were talking to her was *their* problem. In a strange way, however, it was all interesting. Not until she was too sleepy to do anything about it did she remember that she'd forgotten to take one of the white and blue capsules from the bottle the nurse at the Home had thrust into her hand that morning.

The closer Christina came to school, the more slowly she walked. Girls, walking by twos and threes, sometimes a girl and a boy walking together, or a group of jostling boys pushed past her on the sidewalk. No one walked alone.

A yellow convertible with the top down turned at the corner where she was waiting to cross. A girl, with high color and black hair cut like a boy's, was driving. One of the two boys with her in the front seat leaned out and hollered, "Hey, Chris! Want a ride?"

For a second only, Christina allowed herself to hope—and that was long enough. The car pulled to a stop fifteen feet or so ahead and a tall blond boy wearing a blue sweater with a large gold F broke away from the group he had been with and without opening the door of the car stepped into the empty back seat.

Now that she was less than a block from the school, the hundreds of cars that had been converging from all directions seemed to have rather systematically syphoned themselves into an enormous parking area, and were as neatly lined up as toy automobiles in a child's game. Christina could see a stray student or two hurrying up the walk toward the big double doors and vanish inside.

"Better hurry," a voice behind her said. It was a boy, a sturdy-looking boy with thick sandy hair and the face of a leprechaun. He took her elbow as he spoke, propelled her along as one might a rather wayward bicycle. "You're either new or else you've been hiding since school started. I've never seen you before."

"I . . . I'm new." For all of his sturdiness, he was not tall. She had to raise her eyes not more than an inch or two to look into his. Nice eyes of a queer brownish shade. She'd picked up a stone one time, walking on a California beach, of that very shade. Sardonyx, a semi-precious stone, her mother'd said.

"First day?"

She nodded.

"You'll want to go to the office then. Down this hall to your right. I go the other way, but you can't miss. Luck."

The corridor down which she turned to walk was emptying rapidly. When the buzzer rang only seconds later, there was not a soul in sight. Her footsteps echoed in the stillness as she hurried on.

A young woman behind the counter in the office looked up when Christina entered. "I'm a new student," she faltered. "I don't know whom I'm supposed to see. . . ."

"Mr. Bridges is the principal. He's not in his office right now, but you may wait in there if you like."

"I'll come back later," Christina said, knowing it sounded crazy but with such a surge of relief that she did not mind.

"There'll be no need," the girl said brightly. "Here he is now. A new student, Mr. Bridges."

A rotund little man, pink-cheeked with shiny glasses, he beamed on Christina as a father might upon a favorite child. "You'll be Christina . . . er . . . Frederickson. Mr. Keller called yesterday to say you would be enrolling and that he had written your high-school registrar in Spring Valley to send us your grade transcripts. However, we don't need to wait for it to arrive to get you started in your classes. If you'll step in the office, we'll plot a program for you."

Seated on the other side of the big desk, Christina watched fearfully as Mr. Bridges took out a card and began to write.

"A junior in good standing." He smiled. "I'm assuming that. Right? Do you recall your grade average for last year?"

Christina flushed. "B minus. It . . . it would have been better except I'm so terrible in math. It would have been worse if Mr. Finch—he's Geometry—hadn't felt sorry for me because my mother'd died and given me the benefit of the doubt."

Mr. Bridges smiled again. Christina averted her eyes. School principals shouldn't be so smiley. Not when school . . . not when life . . . was so solemn and so serious.

"If you had trouble with second-year math," Mr.

Bridges said, making little scratches on a piece of paper, "I should not assume that you will be wanting to take solid geometry. . . ."

Christina's shudder was so real that this time Mr. Bridges chuckled. "We'll skip math, then, and move on to Social Studies which is required as, of course, is English. For language, I'm guessing French. Right?"

"I like French," Christina said. Her tone sounded more churlish than she intended but Mr. Bridges appeared not to notice. He finished writing and stood up, handing Christina a printed card on which, in a rather illegible hand, he had written her schedule. "We'll see how this works out. I don't think you'll have any trouble finding your way around. And if you do, ask." He walked with her to the door. "Your next class is English. To your right, down the corridor. Social Studies directly above it on the second floor. That gives you an idea. Third period today is an assembly. For that, just follow the crowd. Oh, yes, one other thing. Mr. Tedrow is our Guidance Counsellor. If you should have any problems, you'll find him helpful and understanding. And, of course, I am always available, as is Miss Greenlie, our Girls' Advisor."

Outside in the corridor, the bell rang, but Christina scarcely heard. How much, she wondered uneasily, did Mr. Bridges know about her? Were there overtones of meaning in his last remarks? Would he, Miss Greenlie, and Mr. Tedrow all be watching her? She looked over her shoulder as all up and down the hall doors opened and a tidal wave of students poured down the corridor. Swept along with them, again Christina felt a hand at her elbow. It was the boy with the sardonyx eyes.

"We meet again. Where to, this time?"

"English." She glanced at her card. "Room 108."

"I'll escort you." He grinned. "But no dawdling. When I saw you a little while ago, you looked as if you were taking one step forward and two backward."

There was no time to answer for already he had paused

in front of the door to Room 108. "Sorry to have to turn you over to the infamous Miss Lamb first thing."

"*Infamous* Miss Lamb?" Christina peered in through the open classroom door as she spoke. The woman behind the desk was blond, beautiful, with a face, Christina thought—searching for comparison—of a figurehead on a Viking ship.

"Don't let appearances deceive you. She's a tyrant. But a good teacher. I had her last year. We got along. So will you, if you don't wool-gather in class and get your assignments in on time. Luck."

Christina, watching him as he walked on down the hall could not help but see a girl with swinging auburn hair weaving in and out among the throngs in the corridor, calling "Clay!" as she ran. Not until she had almost caught up with him, did the boy with the sardonyx eyes pause. The girl spoke, the boy named Clay answered. What either said, Christina could not tell. She said the name "Clay" softly to herself, then straightening her shoulders as one about to face a firing squad, went to the infamous Miss Lamb.

Then nothing happened. Or, certainly, nothing bad. Still, she sat there, her clammy hands clasped tightly in her lap, waiting for the axe to fall. She could see what Clay had meant when he'd said Miss Lamb was a tyrant. She asked questions, extracted answers, meted out assignments, including extra assignments for those whose responses or lack of responses displeased her, with the air of a drill sergeant.

"And what of T.S. Eliot?" she cried, in a lull following an excoriation of a huge boy wearing an F sweater who had allowed himself the luxury of a little catnap. "What did T.S. Eliot have in common with Henry James whose short story, *The Beast in the Jungle,* we have been studying the past few days." Miss Lamb's large cerulean eyes scanned the room. "Barbara, what would your answer be?"

As every pair of eyes turned toward the back of the

classroom, so did Christina's. The focus of them all was the girl with the black hair cut like a boy's that Christina had seen that morning at the wheel of the yellow convertible.

"I'm sorry, Miss Lamb, but I don't believe the answer to that question was in our book."

"Sorry!" Miss Lamb's nostrils swelled. "What kind of an answer is that? Of course, the answer isn't in your book. It ought to be in your head. Doesn't anyone know? Doesn't anyone read anything except the few pages assigned to you? Doesn't anyone ever read the newspaper?" Again Miss Lamb's eyes scoured the room. Involuntarily, Christina felt her hand twitch upward.

"You!" Miss Lamb said. "New girl."

"I *think* I know."

"Think!" Miss Lamb said with a snort of scorn. "You either know or you don't know. Which is it?"

Christina felt herself shrinking. Now every eye in the room was on her. "I know this one thing, but maybe it isn't the thing you're thinking about," Christina said faintly. "What I know is that T.S. Eliot was an expatriate. He was an American who went to England to live and became a British citizen. So did Henry James."

Miss Lamb's great eyes rolled upward in supplication. "May the ghost of Henry Wadsworth Longfellow give me strength! Of course, that's the right answer! But why must I go to such lengths in order to pry the answer out of you?"

Little murmurs of laughter, punctuated by an appreciative male guffaw rose from different corners of the room. And everyone was smiling, including Miss Lamb. Everyone, that is, except the girl, with the black hair cut like a boy's, named Barbara. Christina shivered and turned from her cold, green gaze as the bell that ended the class began to ring.

Christina, her hands still clammy, entered the auditorium on a surge of students. The noise of them, two thousand strong, rose and fell like waves breaking on a rocky coast.

A dozen times she saw an empty seat, even a row of empty seats, but all were filled before she could insinuate herself into one of them.

Over the sound of voices rose the thump, thump, thump of drums, the high, intense voices of saxophone and trumpet, the oom-pha-oomph of the big French horns.

Like memory superimposed on a dream, it took her back. She'd loved assemblies at George Washington High in Spring Valley. Then she'd been part of the noise and happiness. Now looking about her, she felt only panic.

The aisles between the seats were almost empty. In a moment, everyone would be seated, the assembly would begin, and she would be standing there alone.

As she looked about her an arm seemed to reach out from nowhere and a voice hissed, "Here's a seat. In here."

A half a dozen pairs of feet were obligingly drawn in as she stumblingly made her way to the empty seat next to the tall, very pretty girl who had rescued her.

With a little breath of thanks, she sank down into the haven of her seat.

"Don't thank me," replied the other. She nodded her head at the pretty girl next to her whose face was almost concealed by a curtain of brown hair. "Thank Trish. She spotted you—though how she can see anything is a mystery. Trish—Letitia, really—Johnson. I'm Trimble Farber. You're . . ."

"Christina Frederickson. This . . . this is my first day."

"Glory!" said the girl called Trimble. "No wonder you looked lost—getting your introduction to Floradale High on the day of a General Assembly."

"But not as bad as the General Assembly when the football season opens." The girl on the other side of Trimble parted her curtain of hair as she spoke.

59

"That's our Trish," said Trimble amiably. "Always looking on the bright side. But she is right. Today's assembly will be tame. Today, they're announcing the new student senate officers—we just had the election yesterday—and we'll hear a few well-chosen words from Mr. Bridges about honor, integrity, the flag, mother. . . ."

"Trimble, don't." Again Trish parted her hair as she spoke. This time she addressed Christina. "Don't pay any attention to her. She just tries to sound cynical and world-weary. Really, she has a marshmallow heart."

"Easy on the commercial," grinned Trimble. "Besides, here comes the great man now."

Someone several rows behind them said "Hush!" With a flourish of drums and a final blare of brass, members of the band laid down their instruments. A shrill, between-the-teeth boy whistle catapulted around the room and a lessening of sound became apparent.

Christina closed her eyes, savoring a sensation that was just next door to happiness. Perhaps if she tried very hard she could be happy again, in spite of everything. The small triumph she had that morning in Miss Lamb's English class had roused in her the almost forgotten feeling of excelling. And' Miss Lamb liked her. Intuitively she had known that. And the boy named Clay. Had he liked her? She could not be sure, but again intuitively, she thought he had. She could still feel in the palm of her hand the electric tingle that the touch of his fingers had generated.

Mr. Bridges was speaking as Christina opened her eyes. He was smiling, his eyes twinkling behind his shiny glasses. "And now we come to the results of the general election yesterday for Student Senate officers. President, Bob Blankman . . . please, no applause until I've given you all the names. Vice-President, Monica Murphy, Secretary, Barbara Jethrow, and Treasurer, Clay Harger."

As Mr. Bridges read off the names, the four walked out on the big stage, bare except for the podium where the principal stood and a row of straight-backed chairs. In seconds, the whole auditorium had become a vast sea of clapping hands.

Trimble leaned toward Christina. "The kids are really clapping for Bob and Clay and Monica. Everybody likes them. But it would take a congressional investigation to figure out how Barb Jethrow got herself elected."

"Scarcely a congressional investigation," Trish said, peering out from her curtain. "She was elected by sycophants. Those who are out and want to be in."

"What she means," Trimble interposed, "is that Barb has her finger in practically every pie in the school—dramatic club, synchronized swimming, Girls' Club—practically everything but the National Honor Society. She's a member, but she doesn't quite control it yet. Moreover, if she gets it in for you, you might as well ship out right now."

"Well, it will at least be interesting to see whether Clay dates her again this year."

"Clay dates?" Christina repeated the words so faintly that Trimble scarcely heard.

"Last year Barb was only one of several girls he went with. This year, I'm betting it will be Barbara all the way." She paused, gave Christina an appraising look. "Say, do you feel all right? You're as green as grass."

"It . . . it's just a little hot in here. I think maybe I'd better go outside."

"I'll go with you," Trimble said.

"Oh, no. Please." Once again the row of feet were obligingly drawn in as she made her way to the aisle and out of the auditorium. She got a drink of water from a fountain a few feet away and had dampened her handkerchief to hold to her forehead when the door opened and Trimble appeared. "You're sure you're all right?"

Christina nodded, so Trimble would go away.

"I could take you to the nurse and you could lie down for a little while."

Christina shook her head, smiled faintly. "I'm all right,

really. It's just a headache." It was true. Scarcely a day passed now without one. "You go back in."

"If you're sure . . ."

"I'm sure." She waited until Trimble had gone back into the auditorium, then quickly and resolutely she walked down the long corridor and out of doors, almost stumbling over a fat girl in an ugly print dress who was sitting on a shallow cement step just outside.

At Christina's absent "Pardon me," the fat girl looked up. With one small part of her mind Christina noticed that her eyes were red-rimmed and her face blotchy from tears. A book of somebody's *Collected Poems* lay open face down beside her. But Christina did not stop. At the end of the sidewalk she paused for a moment then turned, not toward the Kellers' house but in the opposite direction.

CHAPTER SIX

The Old School Try

"You'll have no trouble finding Dr. Fair's office," Dave Keller said. "The bus that goes past your school will take you downtown. Get off at Tenth and Elm and you'll be right in front of the B and H building." He paused to think. "As a matter of fact, I have a half hour between appointments about that time and I could come out and pick you up."

"David, honestly!" Although Mrs. Keller laughed it did not hide her exasperation. "Christina is perfectly capable of finding her way downtown."

Christina stared out of the bus window, not seeing the changing panorama outside but only her own amorphous reflection in the glass. I could say I couldn't find it, she thought. But with such simple instructions that would be hard to believe. Better, to say that Mr. Bridges had called her into his office after school to talk about her grade transcript and that as a result she had missed her bus. By the time another came, the hour for her appointment was long past.

It was not too big a lie. After all, she had had to go

to the office. Not that morning but a week before. And not to Mr. Bridges but to Mrs. Greenlie, the Girls' Advisor.

"You're not getting off to a very good start in a new school, are you?" Mrs. Greenlie's smile was dry. ". . . Cutting classes the first day? If you had gone to the nurse when you felt ill, she would have excused you to go home."

For a moment she thought of telling Mrs. Greenlie the truth; that it wasn't a headache—though she'd really had one—that had made her walk out of school unexcused the day before. It was the girl inside—the only one who really understood—who'd told her what to do. "See!" the girl had said, almost gloatingly. "Nothing goes right anymore. You like a boy—and he likes somebody else. So walk out on him. Walk out on everybody. Go someplace where you can be alone and think things over."

When she'd looked up, she saw that Mrs. Greenlie was still waiting for her to reply. "I didn't know where the nurse's office was," she'd answered defensively. "Everyone was in assembly. There was no one around to ask." Of course, there'd been the fat girl she'd found sitting outside, but she hardly counted—even when Christina discovered the next day she had the locker next to hers.

Mrs. Greenlie smiled a real smile and stamped her name across a pink admitting slip. "We won't make a federal offense out of it this time. As a matter of fact, you don't look as if you felt well today. Perhaps you should see a doctor."

When Christina said she was going to, very soon, Mrs. Greenlie said "good" and let her go.

It was the truth. She *was* going to see a doctor but not the kind of doctor Mrs. Greenlie had in mind.

The bus lurched as it turned onto Elm Street. Nineteenth, Eighteenth, Seventeenth, Sixteenth. No passengers rang to get off. No one stood waiting to get on. Oh, if only it would stop so she could think! If it were Dr. Brandon she was going to see, she would not mind so much—by the time she'd left the hospital, she'd felt that they were almost friends. But Dr. Brandon was not in private practice. With a new psychiatrist, she would have to start from the beginning.

Passengers were alighting at every corner now. Twelfth Street, Eleventh Street, Tenth Street. If someone else rang the bell to go off at Ninth Street, she would get off.

A pretty young woman holding a little girl by the hand got up and stood by the exit before the bus was halfway to the corner. Christina followed them.

Pedestrians filled every inch of the sidewalk in front of the B and H building, but inside the lobby there was no one except the woman and the little girl who had been on the bus. Christina stared at the brass-framed office index on a nearby wall, letting her eyes follow the alphabetized columns until it reached the Fs. The very first name was M.E. Fair, M.D. on the eleventh floor.

When Christina got on the elevator she found the mother and child inside. The button for the eleventh floor had already been pushed. When the cage began to rise, the child began to whimper. The mother bent down. "The doctor won't hurt you, I promise. All he wants is to make you well."

Christina felt tears fill her eyes. Miss Marple had been kind.

When the elevator stopped on the eleventh floor the mother and little girl preceded her down the hall and disappeared into a pediatrician's office. Room 1108 lay straight ahead. "Dr. M.E. Fair, M.D." was printed in block letters on the frosted door. Underneath letters read "Consultation by Appointment Only."

Christina's face grew warm. Why didn't Dr. Fair come right out and say "Psychiatrist"? If there wasn't anything to be ashamed of in going to a psychiatrist, why try to hide it? Walking from the elevator she had passed half a dozen doctors' offices. Each doctor had his specialty—obstetrics, dermatology, urology or whatever—

printed beneath his name, except the great Dr. Fair whose specialty was known by all. It was still not too late to retreat. She could come again another day when she was not feeling so depressed. When she'd had a better day. This day had had nothing to recommend it. Not even a glimpse of Clay Harger in the corridor. During lunch period instead of going to the cafeteria, she had looked in vain for Trimble and Trish whom she had not seen since the day they rescued her in assembly. The only person who wanted to talk to *her* was the fat girl. Every time she went to her locker she was always hanging around.

Her mind, traveling off on this unhappy train of thought, closed her ears to the sound of footsteps behind her.

"Fancy running into the great authority on Henry James and T.S. Eliot down here!" said Barb Jethrow.

Christina twirled guiltily at the sound of the soft mocking voice.

"I'm on my way to the dermatologist myself. Thank goodness, it isn't anything serious. Some horrid fungus I picked up at the swimming pool Dr. Querque says. Have to get rid of it, though, before our synchronized swimming club starts rehearsing for the water frolic at school." Barb Jethrow paused, gave a quick little nod of her head. "Well, you're going in, aren't you? You're not just going to stand there . . ."

"I . . ." Christina began. "I . . ." she repeated, then shaking her head began to cry noiselessly.

"Well, for heaven's sake, don't *cry*," said Barb Jethrow. She sounded honestly surprised. "I didn't *mean* anything. I didn't even *say* anything. Tell me what I said," she demanded.

But Christina was not listening. Head bent, books and purse clutched to her chest, she ran in a broken path toward the elevator.

The front door was locked and Christina opened it with the key that Mrs. Keller had given her that morning. The house had a clean antiseptic smell. She knew without calling out that there was no one there. Their house on Nightingale Hill smelled of lemon verbena. When she'd opened the unlocked door her mother was always there. "I like being here when you get home," her mother said.

She moved silently across the parquet floor as stealthily as if she were a culprit in the dark of night.

When the phone rang, it did so so suddenly and with such intensity that her books and purse flew from her hands, scattering themselves in an untidy arc. Not until the ring sounded for the third time, did Christina take the receiver from the hook.

"I would like to talk to Mrs. Keller, please." The speaker was a woman; her voice was crisp. It was the kind of a voice a receptionist for a psychiatrist would have. At the thought, her heart began beating so loudly it seemed to set up tiny vibrations in the mouthpiece. She held her hand over it, trying to think.

Once, Mitzi had told her that she had been successfully truant from school for almost a month by disguising her voice. "If you hold a handkerchief over your mouth and talk through it, nobody can tell who it is," she'd giggled. "Not even the principal could tell. I just said I was Mom and that poor little Eva was home bad sick."

Christina took a handkerchief out her pocket, held it across her mouth and said "hello" into the receiver.

Her voice to her own ears sounded so strange that it did not seem too surprising that the woman at the other end of the line should have said confidingly, "This is Dr. Fair's office calling. I thought you would like to know that Christina missed her appointment with Dr. Fair this afternoon. Children her age have been known to do almost anything to keep from seeing the doctor, you know."

Always an impossible liar, Christina was to wonder for days afterward how she had managed it. "How very bad of her," she said in a tone that was a proper mingling of dismay and regret. "I'll have Mr. Keller speak to her tonight."

For a moment after the receptionist said "thank you" and hung up, Christina held the lifeless receiver in her hand. Already her elation at the success of her ruse was ebbing slowly away. On the heels of doing one foolish thing that might well have been forgiven her, she had done something else—that could not.

Christina had firmly made her mind up to confess both misdeeds to Dave Keller, but sitting beside him in the car the next morning she could not bring herself to do it. When he came down to breakfast he had said he had not slept well. (Guiltily she, herself, had awakened and had set the table and put on the coffee before anyone else was up.) Nor did he look well. Until her mother's death she had given little thought to the health of anyone older than herself.

"If you wouldn't stay up half the night working," Natalie Keller said. There was a sharp edge of worry in her voice. "You can't hope to get enough sleep when you don't go to bed until two o'clock in the morning."

"Come now! It wasn't that bad. And I did have to get through that material on the Blaise case."

"The Blaise case!" Natalie Keller let her fork fall to her plate. "I'm sick of the Blaise case. Sick of people who exploit you—exhaust your time and energy without the faintest intention of paying you. You haven't said anything to those Blaises, or whoever they are, about a fee, have you? You needn't answer, because I know you haven't."

"Nat, Howard Blaise will pay me if he can. If he doesn't win his case, he won't have any money to pay anybody."

"You're right, of course. But still . . ." Natalie Keller

68

gave a rueful little laugh. "I'm a shrew. Forgive me. It's just that . . ."

"I know." Dave Keller grinned as he pushed back his chair. "Case dismissed. Now anybody riding with me had better start humping."

"Me, Daddy!" Davey, clutching Mr. Hawkins, had appeared suddenly in the doorway.

"Oh, no you're not," said his mother. "You're still in your pajamas and you have your breakfast to eat."

"Christina, I'll see you in the car in five minutes."

She was waiting when he came out, books in her lap, hands clasped around her knees. "I'm glad you decided to ride with me this morning. It will give us a chance to talk," Dave Keller said. He stowed a bulging briefcase in Portia's back seat, then waved at his wife, Davey beside her, standing in the open front door. "I don't make it easy on her," he said.

Christina, beset with her own problems, did not answer. The impulse to confess had been steadily weakening since the night before when she had blurted out that she wanted to go early the next morning.

"Anything special?" he said.

From under downcast lashes, Christina stole a look at the big man beside her. His eyes were focused on the street down which they traveled. His voice had been guileless. Even without telling him, did he know?

She shook her head, unable to add lie to lie.

"You can't hope to make friends in so short a time." He did not seem to be speaking to her.

She held her eyes tightly shut to squeeze back sudden tears. "I know."

"Would you do something for me?"

She looked up, startled. It was the last thing she had expected him to say. "Anything," she said recklessly, then mumbled, "I'll try."

"It won't be that hard. When you get to school this

morning make some inquiries about a club or organization that interests you. Possibly, there might be announcements about some meetings on the bulletin board. Belonging to a club and being active in it is the best way I know to make friends."

In a small voice she said "I'll try" again and slipped from the car when it stopped in front of the school's main entrance.

"You can tell me about it tonight," Dave Keller said casually and with a wave of his hand drove on.

Christina put her sweater and the books she would not be using until after lunch in her locker and walked slowly down the almost empty corridor to the big bulletin board just outside the office. A dozen posters and placards had been thumbtacked to the cork background. Some were gaily illustrated and neatly lettered, others hastily contrived.

"Spinsters' Frolic!" proclaimed one. "Bring a boy and a buck to the Girls' Gym Friday night at 8 p.m."

"Benefit Musical for Kim, Our Korean Orphan! Hear 'The Impossibles,' The Terrible Trio, and the Teeny Boppers' Burlesque! Cast your vote for the group most likely to succeed without trying!" Christina sighed. Such things sounded wonderful, exciting and as far removed from her as happenings on the moon. At home, in Spring Valley, she would be taking Gary Schofield to the Spinsters' Frolic. And most likely, Tim Morton who loved music would ask her to go to the Benefit with him. But she was not in Spring Valley. And she had no home. Self-pity welled within her, flooding her eyes so she could scarcely see the smaller signs and typewritten notices that comprised the rest of the material on the board. Suddenly, she brushed the tears from her eyes. "Coin Club, Now Organizing. Come One—Come All! Little Library 3:40 p.m." Her only coin collection was a half-filled Lincoln-penny book that she had lost interest in as soon as all the easy dates and mint marks had been found. But for her present purpose, that really didn't matter. The announcement of the meeting was signed "Clay Harger."

She opened the door, stood indecisively just inside. She did not see Clay and moved a step backward. It was not too late to retreat for, in fact, none of the half dozen or so boys and girls clustered around one of the study tables at the far end of the room had noticed her. All were listening to Barb Jethrow who, with a mock shudder, said dramatically, "Embarrassed! I could have died! How was I to know where the funny little thing was going? She might have been going to the dentist. There's one right next door. But the minute I said, 'What are you waiting for? Why don't you go right in?' she turned tail and ran as if the devil were at her heels."

A plump girl in a too-tight pink sweater put her hands over her eyes. "Oh, Barbie, how dreadful for you!"

Christina would have turned then and fled, only her legs seemed to have turned into leaden stumps. As she bowed her head, she felt an arm linked through her own and a boy's voice said, "Come on. We'll find chairs together."

She shook her head numbly. "I can't."

"You can," said Clay Harger, giving her arm a little jerk. "Come on."

She walked woodenly beside him, aware of but still only half seeing Barb Jethrow's flushed and embarrassed face, half hearing her nervous laughter as she said, "Oh, there you are, Clay. We didn't want to start until you got here. You're the temporary chairman."

"No, you be. You seemed to be holding everyone's attention when we came in."

"Well, if you insist." Even to Christina's dulled vision Barb Jethrow seemed to have recovered her composure completely.

Another half dozen or so students straggled in and seated themselves at tables and the meeting began to get under way. Christina observed it all as if from a mountaintop. More real was the strong-muscled hand clasped around her own. Once or twice she tried to pull it away but he had only held it more firmly until it lay passive again. Then she was no longer on a mountaintop but on an island, alone with Clay. Far away, on the other side of the water, was Barb Jethrow amazingly visible and audible, organizing the Coin Club. Whatever else she was, Christina thought without rancor, Barbara was efficient. Temporary officers had been elected, a committee appointed to draw up the by-laws, and another to organize a Coin Fair to be held some time in the future. Now a discussion of the faculty advisor was under way.

"I suggest Miss Lamb," Clay Harger said. It was the first time he had spoken since the meeting started.

Barb Jethrow made a face. "Oh, Clay. I don't think we want her."

"You asked for suggestions."

"Oh, well." Barb's glance fell lightly on Clay and then away. "She's all right. But someone might like to suggest someone else."

"I'd like Mrs. Prufrock," said the plump girl in the too-tight pink sweater, anxious to please.

"*I* wouldn,t like *her*." Barb Jethrow's tone was almost rude. She looked around. "We might as well vote on Miss Lamb, then. All those in favor say 'aye.' "

There was a little chorus of "ayes" around the room.

"With that settled," Barb said, "I guess we can adjourn. Next week, same time, same place." She zipped together a notebook lying on the table, tossed her sweater over her arm. Once again, her glance was bright on Clay. "I've my car, Clay. I'll give you a ride home."

Clay stood, pushing back his chair.

Now it is over, Christina thought. The knight-errant has done his good deed. Now that he has shown off in front of everyone he can leave the ugly duckling and ride off into the sunset with the beautiful princess. She now stood, too, smiling wryly at her mixing of cliché and fairy tale.

Clay, too, was smiling. "Thanks, Barb, but my mother let me take her car today, so I'm driving." He paused, grinned, then bent his head in the direction of Christina's ear. "Isn't it ridiculous? Here I'm getting ready to offer you a ride home, and I don't even know your name."

"Christy."

"Christy," Clay said. Nodding approval he tucked her hand in his own again, tossed a · good-night over his shoulder and said, "Let's go, shall we? My name's Clay Harger."

The convertible was a dazzling white with buxom fenders and leather upholstery the color of ripe avocado. The top was down.

"Golly!" Christina breathed the word almost reverently.

"It really is something, isn't it?" Clay slammed the door smartly after Christina was seated, and got in on the other side. "My mother says it brings back the days of her youth. Actually, in her youth she didn't have a car at all. I mean, even her parents didn't. I guess it's because she understands about kids that she lets me take her car as often as she does."

The car growled amiably as Clay slipped it into gear.

"I live in Peony Place . . . if you know where that is."

"Sure thing. That's where that big, old beautiful Victorian monstrosity is. I know, because I'm interested in houses. I'm going to be an architect someday. I hope."

"That house is where I live. It belongs to the Kellers. I stay with them."

Clay nodded, not asking the questions she had been afraid he would ask, saying instead, "I know Mr. Keller. He's great. Best scoutmaster I ever had. There wasn't anything he couldn't do."

Christina said "Yes!" her enthusiasm trailing off as she spoke, for Clay instead of taking a longer way round to Peony Place was taking the shortest route—as in her heart she had known he would do. In seconds the adventure would be over.

He turned the car in between the iron gateposts, drew up beneath the porte cochere. Almost before its wheels had stopped rolling she was out of the car, ready to say brightly, "Thanks for the ride" and run swiftly into the house. But the words did not come out that way at all.

"Thank you for taking pity on me," she said unsteadily. "Thank you for driving me home." Then when she turned to run, she stumbled on one of Davey's toys that had been left in the drive and would have fallen if Clay, already out of the car himself, had not leapt swiftly to her side.

"Hey!" he said, almost roughly. "Where do you think you're going in such a hurry? I haven't asked you . . ."

"Asked me what?" Christina lowered her eyes. "Asked me why I'm living with the Kellers? Asked me what's *wrong* with me?"

"The last part of the question, yes," Clay Harger said. Although he laughed, the hand he placed on her arm as he turned her around was not exactly gentle. "There's something wrong with a girl who won't even give a guy a chance to ask her out on Saturday night, even if she's going to refuse him."

"Ask me out?"

"To the Benefit for Kim, our Korean Orphan, they're having at school. There ought to be some good music . . ." he grinned. "That is, depending on your definition of good. But in any case, will you? Go, I mean?"

"Why . . . why, yes, Clay." Christina smiled. Even in her too-big pleated skirt and sweater, she felt pretty and desirable. "I'd like very much to go with you."

"See you then. And luck."

Although she didn't turn around, Christina knew that Clay stood watching her until the door had closed behind her.

CHAPTER SEVEN

While the Sunshine Lasted

"Chrissie, you're happy." Davey spoke in the loud, clear tone employed when the conversation did not include him.

Christina looked up from her plate, giving the little boy a swift glance. She was surprised that he noticed. Insulated in her own troubles, she rarely noticed him. His round brown eyes, very bright in his thin dark face, were questioning her.

"Why, yes, Davey. I am."

Dave Keller smiled. "You had a good day, then, at school."

Before she could again say "yes," Davey intervened. "But sometimes you're not happy. You cry. At night, Mr. Hawkins and I hear you."

"Everybody cries sometimes," Dave Keller reminded. "Maybe not so you can see or hear. But they cry quietly, inside, because they are unhappy about things that happen in the world."

Excitedly, Davey rose in his chair, bracing his feet against its rungs. "I can cry both ways. I can cry inside and I can cry outside. I can . . ."

"Davey, please. . . ." Natalie Keller said. "And do sit down. You are dribbling gravy down the front of your sweater. After all, no one was discussing you." She laughed to take what might have seemed a tinge of sharpness from her words. "We are happy that Christina is happy. . . ."

Christina flushed. Mrs. Keller had not added "for a change"—but she might as well have, for the aura of the words hung in the air.

The little scene had, however, helped change the subject and Dave Keller steered the conversation back to the topic they had been discussing when they sat down at the table: the rather heated argument her League of Women Voters unit had had that morning over urban renewal.

Christina did not listen. Her mind was busy with every small detail of everything that had happened from the moment Clay had linked his arm through hers and said, "Come on, we'll find seats together," until he had said "good-bye" at the door.

After dinner, she did the dishes and cleaned up the kitchen in less than half the time it ordinarily took her and was on her way upstairs when Dave Keller stopped her. "I didn't want to pursue the subject at dinner—we seemed to have too many things going on—but apparently school went better today?"

"I was going to tell you that . . . tell you that I did what you said. Looked for a club meeting. There was one after school—a new one just getting organized—so I went."

Standing on the second step of the stairway brought her to the level of Dave Keller's interested brown eyes. Momentarily, she looked away. She could not tell him everything, what Barb Jethrow had said and that Clay Harger took pity on her, without confessing the broken appointment with Dr. Fair.

"Yes?" the tall man said.

"A boy was at the meeting and afterward he drove me

home. He says he knows you. His name is Clay Harger."

Dave Keller looked pleased. "I do indeed know him. A fine boy. I had him in a scout troop when he was a little fellow."

"I know," Christina said. "He told me. He thinks you're great."

Dave Keller laughed. "Kids that age find it easy to look up to anyone who can pitch a tent in a high wind, and smaller ones," he added, turning to Davey who was clambering at his knee, "think you're great if you play train with them. O.K., Son, let's go."

Only for a moment did she regret not telling Dave Keller about her date with Clay. But she could do that later. For a while, the knowledge was sweeter in its secretness.

In her room, instead of throwing herself face down across the bed, as she usually did, with her little transistor radio pressed closely to her, listening yet not really listening as the minutes passed, she got at her homework immediately. And instead of staring at each page until the words swam together, her thoughts seemed sharp and clear and the history assignment seemed to do itself. When she reached the halfway point in the work she'd brought home she got up, stretched happily, and took a handful of pencils from the owl mug on her desk and went down the back stairway to the kitchen. A pencil sharpener, cleaned since she had used it last, was fastened to the wall in the butler's pantry. She wound and ground, watching the clean wood shavings mingle with the siftings of the lead as they dropped into the plastic container. When each pencil was stiletto sharp, she started up the stairs. At the landing she paused as the sound of voices came up to her. Davey's was whining, Mrs. Keller's was irritable. Dave Keller's was conciliatory, as always.

"But I *like* reading to David, putting him to bed."

"I know." Impatience, undisguised, colored Natalie

Keller's voice. "But not when you're so tired. Let me read to him tonight."

"No! No! Daddy, read! Daddy! Daddy!"

She smiled and continued up on the stairs. Her father had read to her, too, long after she was old enough to read to herself. *Alice in Wonderland* for one. Not until she was much older and had returned to "Alice" for herself did she discover how skillfully he had skipped the dull parts and woven the interesting parts so carefully together that she, adept as she was at spotting any skipped pages, had never guessed. *Robinson Crusoe, Swiss Family Robinson, Wind in the Willows,* which she knew he'd never liked, he'd read them all to her.

In her room, she again settled happily to work. She had saved the most difficult, but in a way, the most interesting part for the last. Her French assignment was translating a chapter of *Le Petit Prince,* which she loved. And for Miss Lamb, a listing of the principal concepts in *A Separate Peace,* a novel that had both fascinated and troubled her.

As she picked up a pencil and started to work, she heard big David with Davey on his shoulders come galloping up the stairs.

Christina's happiness held until morning. Awakening later than usual, knowing that she should be up and helping, she still allowed herself to be laggard. Perhaps, this once, the Kellers would like to have breakfast by themselves. Whether or not this was true, Mrs. Keller did not seem to mind Christina's late appearance and cheerfully waved her off to school.

The last buzzer was ringing as Christina slipped into her Home Room. Mrs. Fleming, who apparently had already counted her tardy, erased a little place on her record book and made a new pencil mark. Christina noted this with one small part of her mind while the rest of it was busy with what she would say to Clay if she saw him. She had hardly said a word driving home in the car. Thinking back, she couldn't remember saying anything. Still, they must have talked and he must have liked her, at least a little, or he wouldn't have asked her for a date.

The buzzer rang again, then everyone was surging out of the door, Christina with them. A tall, thin boy named Friley Somebody who sat behind her spoke to her as they started down the corridor but she answered absently for a dozen feet ahead of her she had caught a glimpse of Barb Jethrow's sleek black head. In her bright red jersey pullover she could not be missed as she wove her way in and out and disappeared into Miss Lamb's classroom.

The room was already half filled by the time Christina entered. Barb Jethrow was standing at Miss Lamb's desk. "Oh, do please say 'yes.' It's going to be a really great club. Everybody wants you for our advisor. You were simply the unanimous choice of everyone."

Christina could not resist the smallest and most discreet of coughs as she walked by. Barb Jethrow looked up, said, "Oh, hi, Christina," in a tone of complete camaraderie. To Miss Lamb she said, "Christina's in the Coin Club, too."

"I'll have to think it over, Barbara," Miss Lamb said, "but I'm flattered to have been asked."

In her seat at the back of the room, Christina made a little pleat in her lower lip with her fingers and stared thoughtfully at the back of Barb Jethrow's head. At last, the unexpected camaraderie was beginning to make sense. She's afraid I might tattle, Christina thought. She's afraid I might tell Miss Lamb that there was only one person in the Coin Club who didn't want her—and that that person was Barb Jethrow.

Preposterous as the idea was, Christina entertained it briefly. It would really serve Barb Jethrow right for being so cruel, or if not cruel, heartless. But tattling would diminish me, too, Christina thought, and I cannot diminish myself when I am beginning to be whole again.

She opened her book to the proper page a bare second before Miss Lamb said "All right, Christina, let's hear from you."

She didn't own a thing that was right for her date with Clay. Christina went through the dresses in her closet once again. The dress she had counted on wearing, one she loved, an apricot-colored wool, lay in a heap on the floor. A green jumper, with a long-sleeved white blouse, she had not bothered to put back on the hanger. Like the apricot-colored wool, it was hopelessly too big.

If she had any money, she could buy a new dress. Unfortunately, five of the ten dollars Mr. Keller had advanced her until she should start receiving an allowance from her father's estate, had been dribbled away on supplies. If she could sew—her eyes misted as she remembered how her mother had always wanted to teach her— she could buy some pretty material and make one. Or, more practically, if she could sew she could fix the coral-colored wool. She picked it up from the floor, turned it inside out. The sideseams were where it would have to be taken in. But the stitches there would first have to be taken out and they were so hopelessly small that she could hardly see them.

She opened her bedroom door and stood at the top of the stairs and listened to sounds that meant Mrs. Keller was starting to prepare dinner. It was not the best time to ask for help. But unless she wore one of the same sweaters and skirts that she'd been wearing to school she had no choice. Saturday now was but two days away.

Mrs. Keller was peeling potatoes at the kitchen sink when Christina said, "I know you're busy now, but when you have a minute would you help me fix a dress? I'm getting fatter, but still almost everything I own is too big."

"Why, yes, Christina, I'd be glad to." Mrs. Keller looked so surprised and almost pleased that Christina felt a small sense of guilt as she realized that she hadn't really ever talked to Mrs. Keller much at all, even to ask a favor.

"Perhaps after dinner," Mrs. Keller offered.

"That would be wonderful!" Christina's pleasure was genuine although her manner was almost shy. "I met this boy at school and he asked me for a date. On Saturday night."

"Oh, dear, *not* on Saturday. . . ." A small potato dropped with a plop into a pan of water. "If I had known, we might have made plans for another night, but now I'm afraid . . ."

"I already told Clay I would go," Christina said. She looked as if she did not comprehend.

Dave Keller came into the kitchen from the back door as she spoke. "Who's going where?" he asked cheerfully. "Somebody got an invitation?"

"Christina," Mrs. Keller said. "From a boy."

Christina looked up numbly as the big man's arm encircled her shoulder. "That's great! With Clay Harger?"

Stiffly, she nodded. The happiness that until a few minutes before had filled her had ebbed away, leaving her without any feeling at all. Mrs. Keller was still smiling. "It would be great," she said, "if the Gaylords hadn't asked *us* to have dinner with them on Saturday night."

"That shouldn't be an insurmountable problem," Dave Keller said. "We'll get a sitter, the way we always did before Christina came. Get Mrs. Basset. Davey likes her."

"She's gone to California to visit her daughter."

"What about that Treadway girl?"

"I could try her." Mrs. Keller's tone was doubtful.

"I'll pay," Christina said. Her voice in her own ears was thin, unnatural.

"Don't worry about that," Dave Keller's tone was fatherly. "It'll work out. You'll see."

But it didn't seem to. That night, instead of doing her homework she kept making trips out into the hall where, by wedging herself into the corner and hanging rather far out over the stair rail, she could hear Mrs. Keller's, so far, vain attempts to get someone to stay with David. Tears of self-pity leaked from her eyes. If Mrs. Keller didn't find someone soon, she would have no choice but to break her date with Clay. And after that, he would never ask her out again. Christina went back to her room and threw herself across the bed. How cruel life was, and how unfair. If all the terrible things that happened had not happened, she would still be living in Spring Valley. Her mother would already have the material for a new dress spread out on the dining-room table, the pattern laid on, and ready to cut out.

How like the shoemaker's elves her mother was! (She could not bring herself to say "had been.") For always when she awakened the next morning the new dress would be ready for trying on. "But, Mama!" she would cry. "You shouldn't have stayed up so late to work on it!" And her eyes would shine as she looked at herself in the long mirror and held her arms in a little half circle as if she were dancing with a boy. "But I loved doing it—for you," her mother always said, standing back to admire, adding almost shyly, "I always hoped that if I could have but one child, she would be a girl."

When the telephone rang thinly from downstairs, Christina got up and crept silently into the hall. The Treadway girl had not been home when Mrs. Keller had called before. If she was calling now . . . "Please, God," Christina prayed. "Dear God, please let her come."

"Oh, hello, Ann. Your mother said you might be able to stay with David Saturday night. Oh, I see. Well, perhaps another time."

Slowly, Christina began to descend the steps framing her little speech as she went. "Mrs. Keller, don't keep on trying to get a baby-sitter," she would say. "I'll stay. After all you've done for me, I don't mind, really. And I'm sure I can make Clay understand."

Midway down the flight of stairs, Christina paused and gave her head a little shake hoping it might silence the small, insistent voice that was buzzing in her ears. But it did not go away. "What about me?" it said. "Why must I be the one that everything happens to? Wouldn't it better to wait at least another day?"

Christina turned and more slowly than she had descended went back upstairs. After all, there was no need to be hasty. Perhaps, in another day, the problem would solve itself.

School had been out for half an hour when Christina left the library and walked moodily toward her locker. It had not been a good day. Classes had been dull and she had talked to no one. Not even Trimble or Trish who had befriended her that first day in assembly and who always stopped to visit when they saw her. If she had seen Clay, she told herself, she would have broken their date for Saturday night, explaining the best she could. But she did not see him. Now, in all the long corridor there was no one in sight except the fat girl. Christina would have avoided her now if she could, but there was no way. The smell of chocolate was strong in the air as the girl approached, smiling, showing her crooked teeth, her bad complexion.

"I thought we might walk home together," the fat girl said. "At least, part way. I would have tried to catch up with you this morning but you had your head down and I thought that maybe you wanted to be alone."

"I'm not going home quite yet." Christina wondered if her face was flushing with the lie. "First, there's somebody I have to see."

The words were barely out of her mouth when wonderfully, she saw him coming. Smiling, walking faster now that he had seen her.

A flush, deep red, blotched the fat girl's face. "I'll just

go along," she said. "Maybe some other time."

Christina did not even see her go, for the books she had been stacking in her arms to take home tumbled nervelessly from her grasp, sending loose papers flying.

"Here, I'll get that stuff." Clay was kneeling beside her on the floor, his hand reaching for a sprawled book the same second that hers touched it. "Why, you're cold! Your hand's like an ice cube."

She pulled it away, but as swiftly he retrieved it, held it between his two warm ones. He was grinning, flushing a little. "If I could, I'd sing that song from *La Bohème*. You know the one—where Rodolfo finds Mimi the little seamstress freezing in her attic, and sings 'Your Tiny Hand Is Cold'?"

Christina shook her head.

"I guess I'm some kind of a nut," Clay said. He had released her hand, stacked up the books and helped Christina to her feet. "But I love opera. It's so beautiful, but still so . . . so sort of preposterous. A couple of years ago when I was in New York with my parents, they took me to the Met—*Aida* with Leontyne Price, and I flipped. Just plain flipped."

Christina was looking at him wonderingly. What a queer boy he was! His eyes so warm and brown, his cheeks so healthily pink—he was saying, "If I had the car I'd drive you home, but since I don't I guess I'd better be on my way. See you Saturday night about eight o'clock, if not before."

Dully, Christina watched him go. Now that she had had a chance to tell him their date must be broken and had not taken it, life seemed even darker than before.

"If you get the dress you want to wear Saturday night, I'll help you fix it now."

"I . . . I'm not going."

"Have you told Clay?"

Ashamed to face Mrs. Keller, Christina shook her head.

"I was going to call him on the phone tonight."

Mrs. Keller laughed dryly. "Well, your sacrifice won't be necessary. We're not going to the Gaylords after all. . . ."

"Oh, but I didn't mean for you to do that!" Christina said guiltily. "I . . . just hadn't told Clay I couldn't go because I thought maybe you might still be able to get a sitter. I mean, then we could both have gone . . . and I would have paid . . . I would have expected to do that. . . ." Christina's voice trailed off lamely as Mrs. Keller interrupted. "Oh, for heaven's sake, go get your dress and bring it up to the sewing room. I haven't a lot of time before I go to pick up David at the Printemps'."

Christina flew up the stairs on lightning feet, grabbed the coral-colored dress from the floor where it had fallen and was back down the hall to the sewing room. Before Mrs. Keller got there, she had taken off her school dress and put on the coral-colored wool. She stood looking at herself in the full-length mirror on the bedroom door. It was funny, she thought, but the dress didn't look nearly so queer as it had when she had tried it on two days before. And it was really miraculous how just pinning up the hem, as Mrs. Keller was doing now, and taking it in just a little under the arms and at the sides, made her seem to have a little shape again.

"This is really all it needs," Natalie Keller said. Her tone was businesslike but pleased as she stood back to look at the changes the hand-pinning had produced. "It will really look very nice." She had started toward the door when Christina darted toward her. The color that the dress had brought to her cheeks had faded, leaving her bleached-looking. "What do I do now? I might be able to do the hem, but it wouldn't look right . . . and those other places you pinned, what do I do with them?" She was close to tears when Mrs. Keller turned back into the room.

"I don't suppose it's your fault." She seemed to be talking more to herself than to Christina. She took the dress almost absently, sat down, and with a razor blade began to rip the under arm seams. "I'll fix the dress for you this time, but you'd better start learning to do some of these things yourself."

"Oh, thank you! Thank you!" Christina cried. "I'll go and start the dinner. If you like, I'll go get Davey. I can drive . . . I'm a good driver."

"There's a packaged cake mix in the cupboard that I was going to fix," Natalie Keller said. "If you'd stir that up and put it in the oven, then set the table. . . ."

"I'll make icing, too!" Already Christina was out the door. "I can make good icing! It's chocolate and delicious. . . ."

"I can! I can!" Mrs. Keller murmured as she bent over the coral-colored dress. "Just like David . . . but he's only six and she's going on seventeen."

Why the Kellers had decided not to go to their friends, the Gaylords, Christina did not know nor did she bother herself with the reason. Gratitude, she felt, was answer enough. And she showed it by her willing labor. As soon as one job was finished, she presented herself to Mrs. Keller for another.

"You mustn't get too tired," Mrs. Keller said, "but if you'd like you could carry all the sofa cushions from the outdoor porch furniture up to the attic. It's nice today, but this beautiful October weather isn't going to last forever."

The job turned out to be more difficult than Christina expected. Not only were the stairs to the attic steep and narrow, but the pillows so fat and heavy that she could carry only two at a time. Fortunately, the attic itself was so interesting that she could hardly tear herself away after each trip. It was the kind of attic, Christina thought, that you read about in books. Dry, hot, and smelling of long cured wood, it stretched out and around like a vasty, raftered cave. Old furniture, trunks, packing boxes, old-fashioned high-wheeled tricycles, an old crib, a newer crib, an old cradle. Even in the heat, Christina shivered as ghosts of long ago seemed to gather round. Then she gave herself a little shake and headed toward the stairs. If she hurried, she would still have time to wash her hair and dry it outdoors while the sunshine lasted.

CHAPTER EIGHT

"Now That I'm Happy . . ."

"You could sit a little closer. Just to be companionable," Clay said.

Moving like a child, an inch at a time she edged just past the middle of the seat. She lay her hand like an offering between them. Clay gave it a little pat. "There," he said. "That's better," then added, "isn't it?" forcing her to say yes.

Then she laughed because he laughed. For such a short ride, it didn't matter at all where she sat. Already they had traversed the short distance between the Kellers' house and school. At a glance it was easy to see that there was going to be a crowd. Headlights played about in the parking lot, crowds of people streamed through the open double doors.

Clay tucked her hand into his and hurried her along. Inside, in the thronged corridor leading to the auditorium he spoke to almost everyone. And almost everyone, it seemed, knew him. She found herself nodding, too. Heads sometimes turned. Once someone said, "Who's that with Clay?" in a voice loud enough for her to hear.

They found good seats and had barely settled into them when the curtain went up. From then on, the next hour flew. "The Impossibles" were, indeed, impossible and the Terrible Trio terrible. Perhaps even more so, the master of ceremonies explained, as they had a new man playing bongo drums and the group must now be known as The Fearsome Foursome.

At intermission, everyone flocked to the cafeteria for Cokes and doughnuts. Christina, flushed with pride and excitement, was glad when they bumped into Trish and Trimble just inside the door. "Just look at whom we were feeling sorry for the other day," Trish grinned.

There was only one disappointment. Although she sent swift, searching glances to every corner of the big cafeteria and in the corridors on the way back to the auditorium, nowhere did she see the flash of Barb Jethrow's dark eyes or as much as a glimpse of her sleek black hair.

Then during the last half of the show she found out why. Barbara was the principal dancer in the final and best act of the evening, The Teeny Boppers' Burlesque. As Barb clowned and danced her way through the number, Christina felt her early happiness seeping away and by the time the curtain came down, the clapping and whistling had stopped, and the lights came on she felt almost ill. Going out with Clay had not been a victory over Barbara at all.

Allowing Clay to steer her out of the auditorium, she barely answered when a full-throated feminine voice behind her said, "Good evening, Christina. Good evening, Clay."

It was Miss Lamb, looking beautiful, and with a man, Christina noticed, who was piloting her through the crowd as carefully as if she were a tender flower instead of a Valkyrie, almost as tall as he.

After the warmth of the auditorium, the outside air seemed sharp and crisp. Through her thin coat, Christina could feel the warmth of Clay's arm about her as they moved toward the car.

"Barb's having a party at her house for the kids in the show and some others. We can go to that if we want. Or we can go someplace, just the two of us. What do you want to do?"

Christina· shook her head, numbly. "You say."

"It's for the girl to say."

"I'd rather you did." Her tone was dogged, almost ungracious. If she would not say she didn't want to go to Barbara's house, neither could she bring herself to say that she wanted to be alone with Clay.

Clay grinned. "That makes the decision easy, because I'm going to be a dog in the manger. Let's go to the Leaning Tower for a pizza. It's really kind of a funny little place, but the food is good and it's quiet so we can talk."

Clay had no sooner spoken than Christina knew it would have been better to go to Barbara's house after all. There she could have found a quiet corner, let herself be invisible. Alone with Clay she would have no way of protecting herself. People got acquainted by asking questions, exchanging answers. She put a finger to her lips, tore at a shred of fingernail. She could see his expression change when he found out about her, feel his withdrawal.

"Don't bite," said Clay.

Guiltily, she turned toward him but he kept his eyes on the swift moving pattern of traffic in which they were traveling. "Pardon me?"

". . . your fingernails," he finished. "I couldn't help noticing." She made her hands into fists, stared at them.

"You're not mad?"

She shook her head.

"I'm glad. But you never know. Sometimes I think I don't understand girls at all."

"And I don't understand boys," Christina thought. "At least, not this boy." She no longer felt guilty, but was happy again. Moreover, something was happening that hither-to she had hardly been aware of. For at least the second time, and perhaps the third, they were traveling past the same downtown street corners. The same car, a black Pontiac, that had been ahead of them when they had turned into the thoroughfare was ahead of them still. And the same cars—a beat-up station wagon and a red Mustang—were still abreast of them in the traffic lanes to the left and the right of their own.

"Just looping the loop," Clay said, reading her mind. "It's the greatest Saturday night game in Floradale. Any kid who's lucky enough to get his hands on a car drives downtown to see what's going on. Usually, nothing much is. But you see kids and kids see you. It's a harmless enough sport if you don't let yourself fall for any drag racing. And there's no future in that. The cops keep a pretty sharp eye out. On the other hand, as long as kids behave themselves, they've no objection to the kids riding around." Clay turned onto a side street as he finished speaking. "I guess that fulfills our obligation. Now for something to eat."

Less than five minutes later Clay was parking the car in a small private lot and pointing out the large sign painted on the side of the building that adjoined it.

"Parking for Leaning Tower patrons only.
All others will be PERSECUTED."

"I finally got up the nerve to ask the fellow who runs it if the slip was intentional. And, of course, it was."

A bell tinkled as Clay pushed open the door, allowing Christina to precede him into the restaurant. It was not as small as she had expected, nor as quiet as she had feared. A dozen or more late diners still sat at the small tables with the red-and-white checked tablecloths, laughter and the murmur of voices came from the row of high-backed booths along one side of the long narrow room. And best of all, there was the sound of music—coming from an oversized, garishly lighted juke box, to be sure—and a square of dance floor at the moment unoccupied.

A handsome man of middle age, blue-eyed and fair-skinned, appeared, was introduced to Christina as Angelino Fermi, the proprietor. In the booth, in which Angelino left them after taking their orders, Clay once again seemed to divine the question in her mind. "Until I met Angelino, I thought all Italians had dark hair and swarthy complexions. And I thought all Italians not born in the United States talked like old Dominic who helps my mother with her garden. Crazy, man." Clay laughed at himself. "I was too stupid to know that Italians from the north of Italy are generally fair. Angelino, it happens, didn't come to the United States until he was twelve, yet he speaks as good English as I do. In other words, I guess you can't tell what's on the inside of the package by looking at the outside."

Christina looked up sharply. Was there a hidden meaning in Clay's seemingly innocent remark? There was no time to wonder about it for Angelino himself, was back with their pizzas. Oozing with melted cheese, spicy sausage, not just little islands here and there, but spread thick across the top, the fragrance was almost paralyzing. Not until each was more than half through, was there time for much more than monosyllabic conversation. Then someone changed the record on the juke box and music so irresistible filled the restaurant that Clay held out his hand.

"We fit," she thought contentedly, as Clay's arm went around her. He was not so tall that her only view was that of the lapel of a tweedy jacket; nor so short that she had to condense herself to make her head even with his own. When he held her close it was as if each had become a part of the other. When the music stopped, the two or three other couples who had been dancing had left the floor and they were alone. A little scattering of polite applause came from around the room as they went back to the booth.

Christina shivered slightly but Clay had noticed.

"If you don't want any more to eat, let's go," he said.

This time she sat close beside him without prompting. He did not put his arm around her as he drove but there was no need. Except for the quiet purring of the motor and the faint music from the radio sounding so far away that it might have been coming from another planet, there was no sound between them.

She did not know where they were going but they were not going home. That was the important thing.

"I'm going to tell you something—maybe I shouldn't, but I am—because I think a lot of trouble comes from people not being honest with each other."

"Tell me . . . what?" Like a small creature sensing danger, Christina turned toward Clay. She was not at all sure she wanted to know what he was going to say.

"You looked so beat and forlorn that day of the Coin Club meeting when Barb Jethrow started sounding off about you, I felt I had to do something. That's why I offered to drive you home. I asked you for a date for the same reason. Now I feel that Barb did me a favor."

It was a queer kind of compliment, Christina thought, but she was grateful for it. "I'm glad you asked me—whatever the reason."

The car had been ascending a winding road as they talked but not until Clay brought it to a stop on top of a high plateau and she saw the lights of the city winking like a hundred thousand fireflies in the distance, did she realize how high they had come.

Clay turned off the motor. "On a map, it's called 'High Point.' Descriptive, but not imaginative. Every couple of years or so, some nut crawls out on the other side of that barrier and jumps. Have to pick up the remains in a basket. There's nothing but rocks below."

Christina shuddered, put her face in her hands. "Don't.

I don't want to hear any more."

"I know. It's terrible. But what I can't understand is how a person could do it. Take his own life, I mean. Not unless he hated everybody in the world, and himself worst of all."

It was so dark in the car that Christina could not see his face. Her heart started pounding. What had he heard about her? She forced herself to speak. "What . . . what do you mean?"

"It's hard to put in words," Clay said slowly. "But instead of hating, a person must love. Instead of giving up, he must persevere. Be brave. As brave as you are." He did not wait for her to speak but blundered on. "I . . . I'm afraid I took advantage of my job. I work after school three days a week for Mr. Bridges. File correspondence, do some typing. After I'd asked you for a date, I looked up your file . . . found your grade transcript and a letter from your principal to Mr. Bridges telling about your mother and how hard it had been for you after she died. He said your grades had gone down some but that you still finished the year all right." Clay shook his head. "Then to come here, start in at a new school during your junior year—that takes guts."

"You think *that* takes guts?" She asked the question, then began to cry. "You don't know that three months after my mother died my . . . my father was . . . killed in an automobile accident."

"Oh, my God!" His voice dropped to a whisper. "You poor kid. You poor little kid."

She lay back against his chest, letting herself be comforted, yet thinking. If she found the words to tell him all the sad and sordid rest, would he understand how she had felt the night she left Aunt Henriette's house for the last time? Or would his understanding stop at that? Would he turn away, think her some kind of "nut"—like those people who crawled out beyond the barrier on this very point of land and leaped to the rocks below?

She closed her eyes as Clay's arm tightened around her shoulder. "All that happened in the old life. You have a new life now." His voice was husky.

"I'm trying." There were still tears in her eyes but she felt brave now and not sad at all.

He tipped her face toward his. "Could I . . . would you care if I kissed the Christina with the new life good-night?"

For answer, Christina turned toward him.

Clay straightened first. "I think I'd better take you home. I don't want to make the Kellers sore the first night I take you out."

At home when she fumbled with the key in the lock, Clay took it from her hand. The door swung open and he stepped back. "I'll see you around school on Monday. And next weekend, either Friday or Saturday night if you're not busy. . . ."

"I'd love to. But this time, I think I'd better check with the Kellers first."

"Good idea."

She had given him a version, if not an exact account, of the mix-up with the Kellers and he was smiling. "You can let me know. If they've made plans, we'll go another night."

The moment she nodded he was gone, running down the steps and across the yard, clearing the hedge with a jump. She watched until the car was out of sight down the drive then closed the door behind her.

The light was on in the downstairs study and the green-shaded double student lamp cast a soft glow into the hall. Dave Keller looked up from his desk.

"Christina?"

"Yes?"

"If you're not too tired to talk for a few minutes would you please come in?"

"I . . . I'm not tired." Filled with a vague uneasiness

when he had first called out to her, her uneasiness was now increasing with every beat of her heart. With his glasses on, Dave Keller always looked more severe.

"You might want to sit down," he said.

She perched on the edge of a captain's chair, stared down at the toes of her shoes, then flicked a glance toward the big man on the other side of the desk.

When he asked gravely if she had had a good time, the word "Wonderful!" burst from her too loudly, almost defiantly. She flushed.

Dave Keller's smile was faint. "I thought you would enjoy yourself. That's why I told my wife that I didn't feel up to going to the Gaylords' tonight—though I don't think I convinced *her* that was the reason. That's why I also didn't say anything about this matter before you left on your date with Clay. I was afraid it might spoil a pleasant evening."

"I don't know what you mean." But she did know what he meant. She could see the letter now, lying face up on the desk; could read the neat black letterhead, M.E. Fair, M.D.

"The letter came today," Dave Keller said. "To my office. Perhaps you'd like to read it."

"I can't!" she cried. "Don't make me!" She buried her face in the bend of her elbow.

"I won't make you. There's no need for you to read it anyway. You know what the letter says. First, that you didn't keep the appointment I made for you and second, that a certain telephone call to my wife from the doctor's office was rather mysteriously answered by an . . . impostor."

"I'm sorry! I meant to go to the doctor. I did go. Then I ran away. When . . . when I came in the house that day, the phone was ringing. I answered it . . . said what I did without thinking. Afterward, when I wanted to tell you everything . . . remember, that morning in the car I tried . . . you do remember, don't you?" Christina jumped up, circled the desk, and kneeling on the floor grasped the arm of Dave Keller's chair as fiercely as if it were a life raft in a stormy sea. "The longer I put off telling you, the harder it got. And then . . . then I convinced myself it didn't matter any more."

"It matters to me only, Christina, because I want you to be well and happy."

Not until his fatherly arm was around her shoulder and her nose buried briefly against the tweedy, tobacco-ey jacket and she knew she was forgiven, did she dare to let her spirits rise. "Now I won't need to go to the doctor! Now that I'm happy, I'll be well." She took a step back, twirled the skirt of the coral-colored dress. "Oh, you'll see how well and happy I shall be! Tell me I don't have to go to the doctor any more! Promise me!"

"I can't promise you that." Though he had been smiling, his face was grave again. "Judge Rick made the recommendation. I can't change it. And when Miss Stevenson makes her visit to see how you are doing, she'll have to know."

"We'll just wait a little while and see, shall we? It won't do any harm to wait a week or two or three. Please?"

Dave Keller stood, a tall, stooped man, his voice suddenly weary. "In any case, we won't decide anything tonight."

"Thank you! Thank you!" Christina cried. "I promise you, you won't be sorry."

CHAPTER NINE

The Siren Sound

No one could remember such an October. Hard maples, oaks, and sumac burned with crimson and gold on every hillside; flowers bloomed as madly as they had in June. Every day the sun shone and Christina was happy.

In a little more than two weeks Christina could see the difference in herself. The dark half-moons beneath her eyes had disappeared. Her hair, which only a short while ago had been as lifeless as her spirit, now bounced as she walked, unfurled itself behind her like a pale silken banner when she ran to meet Trish or Trimble or other new friends that she'd made through the Coin Club. Astonishingly, Barb Jethrow had asked her to serve on a committee.

Kids who had never noticed her before said hello in the halls. Her mind seemed sharper, more able to cope with the work the teachers were assigning now that the school year had really gotten down to business. And in some way she did not quite understand, she and Miss Lamb had become friends.

The catalyst for her happiness was Clay. Although

some days she did not see him—three afternoons a week he was working in the office after school—his absence only seemed to heighten the quality of her happiness when he appeared suddenly at her locker saying, "I'm mobile. Meet me outside the library after school and I'll drive you home."

That they'd only had two real dates—to the talent show and a week later to a movie, doubling with Trimble Farber and a boy named Maurie Wolfson who rather resembled Mr. Hawkins—did not matter at all. She hadn't even minded that on one occasion when Clay asked her for a date the Kellers had also made plans. That evening he called and played the whole score of *La Bohème* to her over the telephone. Even though her eyes had misted over when Rodolfo sang "Your Tiny Hand Is Cold" to Mimi, they were happy tears that left no trace.

Dave Keller said no more about making another appointment with Dr. Fair, nor did Miss Stevenson who appeared one afternoon after school at the wheel of the black Plymouth. Miss Stevenson, beautiful and efficient as ever, simply asked questions, nodded approvingly and looking, Christina thought, rather pleasantly surprised, went on her way.

Every day the old life slipped farther and farther into the shadows. Sometimes when she stopped to look, she could see her mother and her father standing hand in hand surrounded by the vague trailing mists of the other world. But rather than let herself be ravaged by guilt and grief she would turn her face the other way. When she awakened in the night, as she sometimes did when Davey cried out and she heard Mrs. Keller moving swiftly down the hall to his room, her heart would pound with terror because her parents had been forgotten and she had betrayed them.

Curiously, the solution which came so easily and worked so well would never have occurred to her if the fat girl had not been lurking in the hall one morning when Christina came to school.

Usually, when Christina ignored her—not really ignored her, Christina told herself, because she always *was* in a hurry and there wasn't time for a lot of idle talk—the fat girl took a library book and candy bar from her locker and faded away down the hall.

This morning the device was not going to work. Christina could tell at a glance. The fat girl, looking really worse than usual in a mustard-colored dress, had a flushed determined air that Christina had never been aware of before. Or, perhaps, Christina thought in a moment of rare candor with herself, she had never really been aware of her as a person at all but only as a large, unhappy object that was always standing about wanting to talk when she was in a hurry.

"That parent-teacher workshop here at school Friday night," the fat girl said, "are your parents going?" She had come close to Christina to ask the question and her breath was cloying with the smell of chocolate.

"The what?" Christina said. Already she had turned away and was getting something from her locker, when she suddenly remembered the posters she'd seen in the halls. "Oh, that," she said, then added swiftly, "No. No, they're not. They . . . they'll both be out of town."

"Oh," the fat girl said. She seemed to shrink a little. "I only wish mine were. They'll be here all right—only at the parent-teacher workshop at Tech High where my brother goes. He's the first boy on either side of the family in two generations and they still haven't got over the shock." She shrugged. "Not that it matters. Not that anything does." Her face had a queer flushed look and for a moment Christina thought she was going to cry, instead she walked away.

Christina considered running after her but already the mustard-colored dress had disappeared around the corner. There was little she could have said or done anyway, Christina decided. Besides, her mind was already turning over the thought which she had so inadvertently expressed

101

to the fat girl. That night after she had gone to bed she was almost ready to convince herself that it was true. After all, her parents really could be away on a trip. A long trip, perhaps around the world. They *had* always wanted to travel. Her father had told her once that he wanted to be a foreign correspondent. "In fact, I might have been," he told her once, "except that then I would have hardly ever seen my little girl." Instead, when his father died, he'd given up his newspaper job and they'd all moved back to Spring Valley and he'd taken over the factory. So it was only fair that he should be traveling now and that her mother go along.

She had been in bed, but she had got up and turned on the light on her desk. There was a map of the world in her history book. She shut her eyes, drew a series of circles with her finger in the air then put it down. Karachi! She could not, she decided, have made a better choice.

"Yes, they're in Karachi," she said aloud. "My father's gathering material for a book."

She turned off the light and slipped back into bed. It was so much nicer thinking about them alive and well than . . . than . . . dead. Some day, but not for a long time yet, they'd come home and then they would all be reunited and live happily ever after.

She was surprised that Clay looked at her so strangely when she told him.

"But they are dead," he said. "Making up a fairy tale about them won't bring them back to life."

"But it doesn't hurt anything," she'd argued. "It . . . it's just pretend. Davey pretends all the time. That he's an airplane pilot, that his teddy bear can make himself invisible by pressing a little bare spot on his wrist."

"But Davey's a child and you're grown up. Or almost, anyway. Being grown up means facing things—facing things the way they are, not the way you want them to be."

"I only want to be happy . . ." Leaning against him in the shadows of the porch, looking into his eyes she could see the little star shapes of reflected light. ". . . As happy as I am now."

He tipped her face closer to his. "If only I were older . . . through school."

She let him kiss her once then drew back.

"Don't go in yet. Please."

"But I must." She broke away once again and had the front door open before he reached her. "Good night, dear Clay. Good night."

Inside the house she leaned with her back against the door. From the light at the far end of the hall she could see her reflection in the pier-glass mirror near which she stood. For a moment she let the girl inside smile back at her approvingly then she sped lightly up the stairs.

She was walking home from school the long way and had stopped in Peterson's Drugstore when she saw him. There could be no doubt that it was he. No one else she knew had that curious slouch as if the one hand now thrust into the pocket of his hip-huggers had permanently lowered his right shoulder. No one else had hair that color—neither blond nor brown but a muddy mingling of the two, nor such bold staring eyes.

She simply looked up from the piles of notebook paper, folders, and binders stacked near the window and there he was. On the outside of the building looking in.

Coldness crept into her hands. She dropped the packet of paper that she held, moved back into the interior of the store. The soda fountain, at least, offered some protection. Jammed as it always was after school, there were two or three people waiting for every stool, the boys showing off with loud laughs and wisecracks, the girls squealing, while two harried clerks scurried up and down behind the counter mixing Cokes and grilling sandwiches.

Here in the jostle of kids he could not see her. But when the crowd thinned out or if he came in the store he would find her. And when she left, he would be waiting.

Her heart was pounding so she scarcely heard the voice behind her say, "Buy you a Coke, Christina."

It was Maurie Wolfson who'd been with Trimble the night Clay had taken her to the movie. She forced herself to smile so her dimple would appear, made herself her most appealing "Thanks, no. But if you've a car you could drive me home."

"Sorry. Another time."

"Thanks anyway. I . . . I have to get a prescription filled." Already she was drifting toward the back of the drugstore where a man wearing a white pharmacist's coat stood behind an open window. (He was as old as her father, now living in Karachi. Perhaps even older.)

She managed a dimple. "Is . . . is there a back door? Another way I could go out? There's someone waiting outside that . . . that I don't want to see."

A smile twitched at the corner of the pharmacist's mouth. "That is a dilemma. Under the circumstances, I don't see why not. Here, you can come through this way."

Almost blindly she followed the starched jacket through what seemed a maze of packing cases. Bottles of colored fluids winked at her from their shelves. Mingled with the faint medicinal smells was the cloying scent of cosmetics. She had begun to feel light-headed, almost ill, by the time the pharmacist opened the heavy metal door at the rear of the store.

"If you cut through that back yard there," he said, pointing, "you'll come out on Glover Street. You can take it from there. Good luck."

She began to run, skimming across the cindered parking area at the rear of the store, through a hedge, into a grassy back yard. Two little children playing in a sandbox dropped pails and shovels and watched as she darted past them and around the corner of the house.

Her heart pounding, her shoes slapped on the sidewalk in an offbeat rhythm. A misty trail of darkness flowed before her eyes. Not until she was a block from Peony

Place did she stop running. As far as she could see, there was no one behind her. Only a bread truck passing down the street disturbed the quiet crispness of late October afternoon.

As her panic dissolved, a trace of doubt began to insinuate itself into her mind. Could that face at the window not have been that of Leo Cole after all? How much better it would be to believe that it was only someone who looked like him.

That evening by the time Clay called to take her to the little-theater performance of *The Beggar's Opera,* she had pushed all thought of Leo Cole into the dark recesses of her mind, then, for days, she was too happy to think about him at all.

Was it her own, or another's cry that had awakened her? She sat up in bed in the darkness holding a clutch of sheet to her chest. When the cry came again, she knew that it was Davey's. There was the soft pat-pat of slippered feet in the hall outside her room. A door opened and closed and once again there was silence. She lay back waiting for the little pulses in her throat and forehead to cease their throbbing. Minutes passed before the tapping she had only half heard grew louder. Even then she did not realize that the door to her room had opened until in the dim light from the hall she saw Natalie Keller. Ghostlike in her long, white robe, she moved cautiously into the room. When she whispered, "Christina, are you awake?" even her voice was so unnatural and afraid that Christina, answering, heard a tremor in her own voice.

"Go stay with Davey. He's asleep now, I think, but I don't want him to wake up, not find me there and start crying. I'll go back to Dave. He's not feeling well. I've already called the doctor. He . . . he's on his way."

Christina scrambled from bed. Without turning on the light she found slippers and a robe.

"There's a cot in Davey's room. Perhaps you can get

105

some sleep in there." Mrs. Keller spoke from the doorway.

Davey was asleep. In the glow of the small night light she could see him. One arm was flung over his head. The other arm that had been holding Mr. Hawkins hung loosely over the side of the bed.

Davey knew he was too old for Mr. Hawkins, but he loved him still. Christina picked up the teddy bear. The bear's face, which she pressed against her own cheek, was still damp with the little boy's tears. For a moment she held Mr. Hawkins tightly, then put him back beside Davey, tucking the cover in around them both.

There was a quilt on the foot of the cot. Christina wrapped it around her, Indian fashion, then settled herself sideways in the window seat and looked out into the night. As her eyes accustomed themselves to the darkness she could see the sweep of shrubbery that followed the curvings line of the driveway. An owl with great spreading wings floated across her line of vision and disappeared. So mournful, moody, and beautiful, it was so like a vast stage setting that she would not have been surprised if a hidden orchestra had begun to play the opening bars of *Swan Lake* and the *corps de ballet,* dressed in their feathered tutus, had entered on toe-point from the wings.

Instead, the headlights of a car flashed up the driveway and the illusion was dispelled. Brakes screeched, a car door slammed, and a man ran swiftly toward the house.

She went to the door of Davey's room and watched as the doctor, short and powerfully built, his bag banging at his knees as he ran, preceded Natalie Keller down the hall and into the master bedroom.

Christine huddled at the foot of the cot. Until she had seen the doctor running she had not been afraid. Now as the wail of a siren that she had first heard in the far-off-distance drew closer, uneasiness flowed through her like a sickness. She bit hard into the knuckle of a forefinger, yet did not feel the pain as the ambulance turned into the drive.

Less than seconds later Mrs. Keller, dressed now, was standing at the door of Davey's room. "I'm going with him to the hospital. Take care of Davey until I get back."

She watched, as if mesmerized, from the window as the shadowy figures of the white-coated attendants, Mrs. Keller, and the doctor following, carried the stretcher with its heavy burden down the steps and slipped it into the widespread doors at the rear of the ambulance.

Scarcely was it out of sight down the drive when sudden clouds scudded across the heavens, erasing the face of the moon. A rising wind tossed the branches of the oaks and maples, scattering leaves that almost overnight had turned sear and brown. But not until a spatter of raindrops flung themselves against the window and ran like tears down the pane, did Christina know that the long autumn was over and winter had come at last.

CHAPTER TEN

Idols of the Cave

Davey, smearing finger paint on a piece of butcher's paper stretched the length of the kitchen, sat back on his heels when he reached its end. Pleased, he surveyed his handiwork. It was an ocean full of monsters. No, it was a sky full of creatures! "Look! Chrissie!" he cried. "Look at what I painted!" His exuberance faded as he spoke. "Chrissie, what do *you* think it is?"

Christina gave the painting an absent look. "I don't know what it is, but it's very nice."

"I'm going to let you have a turn now." The little boy's voice was gravely polite.

"You can have my turn," Christina said. "Big girls don't finger paint."

"Big boys don't finger paint, either. I . . . I don't think I want to do it any more."

Christina did not answer but wadded up the sheet of paper and rinsed out the pan of finger paint. She had known when she got out all the equipment that Davey would not be amused for long but the morning had to be gotten through, somehow. And it was not yet nine o'clock.

If it had not rained, Davey might have gone to school but with a cold that had kept him home two days earlier that week, she had not dared let him go. Not, at least, until his mother called saying it would be all right. And Davey not being in school, meant that she was not in school either. She wondered if Clay had yet discovered that she was absent. When he found out, would he worry?

The sudden ringing of the phone jerked her to her feet like a puppet pulled by a hidden string.

It was not Mrs. Keller, however, as Christina had prayed it would be, but her friend Liz Printemps. A tall, handsome woman with the ringing dramatic voice of one trained for the theater, she had made Christina feel overpowered on the one occasion they'd met. It seemed too much now to have to be explaining why she wasn't in school, why Davey wasn't in school, and all that had happened the night before.

Yet there was no doubt that the shock in Mrs. Printemps' voice was genuine once she had the answers to her questions. "It really doesn't look good, does it?"

"I don't know what you mean. . . ."

"Obviously it's his heart. This is his second attack, you know. And he has been warned."

"I . . . I didn't know. . . ."

"No, I guess you wouldn't," Liz Printemps said.

There was an overtone in her voice that would have been distressing if Christina had had time to think about it, but Liz Printemps was talking again, offering to take care of Davey, do anything at all that would be helpful.

Christina said that she was expecting Mrs. Keller to call any minute and that she would give her the message, but the morning dragged by and the telephone did not ring. Christina fixed lunch which neither she nor Davey ate, and a little later he fell asleep, in his father's big chair in the library, watching television.

Too nervous to study, even to read, Christina moved like a wraith through the big silent house waiting for something, anything, to happen. Yet she was so wrapped up in her own unhappy thoughts that not until she saw the front door open did she know that Mrs. Keller had come home. The doctor was with her.

Running toward them, Christina slowed, then stopped. Natalie Keller's eyes were red-rimmed but her voice was composed. "Don't ask me how he is, Christina. There's no need."

"Mr. Keller died about an hour ago," the doctor said gently. "Now I'm going to see that Mrs. Keller gets some rest."

The rain continued through the day of the funeral. By now, Christina almost welcomed it. The soughing of the wind, the sodden sky, the incessant drip, drip, drip of the rain seemed a proper accompaniment for her spirits.

The procession of people through the house—friends, relatives, neighbors—never seemed to end. And with almost every person there came food and flowers: cakes, pies, pans of cookies, casserole dishes, baked hams, meat loaves and salads. When the freezer was full, Liz Printemps took things home to put in her freezer until Natalie Keller should need them.

That seemed like never. Relatives went home. Davey, who had gone to stay with his Grandmother Murdoch, would not return for another several days. Natalie Keller ate only from duty and Christina, not at all. Sleeping again became a problem and Aunt Henriette once more started appearing in her dreams. Once, in a dream, she went to answer the front door only to find her Aunt and Leo Cole standing there.

When she returned to school the skirts and sweaters she had started to fill out properly were once again hanging in their old loose folds.

Clay, who was waiting for her at her locker after school the day she came back, was too startled to be tactful. "You look as if you've been run through a wringer," he

111

said flatly. "Backward. What happened?"

"I . . . I thought you knew. Mr. Keller . . . died."

"I know. It really shook me. I tried to call you the night I read it in the paper, but the line was always busy. That's why I decided I'd just better write you a note. You got it O.K.?"

"It . . . it was sweet." She found a little wad of tissue in her purse and dabbed at her eyes.

"Listen," Clay said roughly. He darted a quick glance over his shoulder to see if anyone was coming down the hall. "You've got to stop this. Sure, it's too bad. Dave Keller was a nice guy. But after all, he wasn't your father. He's not even your uncle. And if he was, it wouldn't make any difference. What's happened has happened. That's just the way it is. And you can't change any of it by feeling sorry for yourself."

"You don't understand!" Her eyes were blurring so she could hardly see him. "You have a mother and a father and all kinds of brothers and sisters. Since Mr. Keller died, I haven't anybody . . . anybody at all."

Clay flushed uncomfortably, thrust a large white handkerchief in her direction. "Maybe I shouldn't have said anything, but I still think . . ."

"Clay. . . . please?" Her eyes implored him.

"Sure thing." Though his voice was gruff the pressure of his arm was gentle as he propelled her down the hall, away from a group of approaching students, and out of doors. "We'll go for a little ride and then I'll take you home. O.K.?"

She gave him a grateful glance. During the three days just past, she had washed thousands of dishes, gone on a hundred errands, and no one had paid any attention to her. Not that she wanted praise for a single thing that she had done—she owed the Kellers more than she could ever pay back—but if she could not make Clay understand what she'd been through there was no point in going on.

He put her in the car, got in on the other side. "The

heater works fast. It will be warm as toast in here in a minute."

She let herself lean against him, feeling little electric particles flow from his strong boy-body into her own.

"A lady never show signs of her affection in public," her mother always said when she saw a young couple walking each with an arm around the other on a city street. But Christina did not care about that now. She drew in a sad little whimpering breath. She needed Clay. Needed his strength and his love. With the heavy home-bound traffic swirling about, no one was noticing them at all.

By the time Clay drew up in the Kellers' drive, lights were winking on up and down the street.

Clay didn't kiss her but gave her hand a hard, almost brotherly squeeze. "I want you to go to bed tonight and sleep about fourteen hours. Things will be better tomorrow and the next day they will be better still. And for crying out loud, start eating again. Dinner tonight and breakfast tomorrow morning. O.K.?"

"I'll try."

"Don't just try. Do it. Promise?"

She watched the small car roar away down the drive and walked slowly toward the house.

Natalie Keller was in her husband's study, sitting in his chair. She looked up when she heard Christina, let her glance flicker across the face of the clock on the desk.

"Davey's coming home tomorrow, so we might as well get some things settled now," she said, "if you've time to talk."

Christina crept into the room. Now it was coming—the thing that she had so feared that she had not even let the thought take substance in her mind. With David Keller's death, the arrangement the court had made for her would be terminated. There would be another hearing—and this time perhaps Aunt Henriette would win.

Natalie Keller looked up from the papers spread about

113

her on the desk. "I've been offered a job at Larkin's Dress Shop. If we can work things out, I'll start next Monday morning."

"I . . . I don't understand."

"A job, Christina. I'm going to work. Even with a B.A. degree, I'm afraid that's about all I'm equipped to do right now. Besides the salary there'll be commissions. Everything will help."

Whether Mrs. Keller's eyes were frightened or defensive, Christina did not know. Still coping with her own sense of shock, she looked away.

"I can drop Davey off at school on my way to work, but as I won't be getting home until six, I have to make some provision for him after school. So, if you'd like to stay on and if Judge Rick is willing, under the circumstances, to let you . . ."

"I . . . I'd like to stay."

"Then that's settled," Natalie Keller said. Composed, she once more turned to the papers before her on the desk. "You'll find almost anything you want to eat in the refrigerator. I'll have my dinner later on, on a tray here in the study."

Christina went to the kitchen, looked unseeingly into the refrigerator and then closed it without taking anything. In her room, she threw herself face down upon the bed, listening for Davey's high-pitched voice crying, "Read me, Daddy!"; listening for Dave Keller's deep-throated, happy response, for the scamper of feet on the stairs. But in all the big, old house there was no sound at all. Tears leaked from her eyes, soaked into the tufts of the candlewick spread, and left no trace. When the phone rang she got off the bed and moved toward the door knowing it would be Clay. For Clay was the only person in the world who now cared at all.

But if it was Clay, why did Mrs. Keller not call her? She hovered over the banister, silent in her stocking feet, moved down several steps.

114

"Oh, Liz!" Mrs. Keller said softly from the hall below. "No, she can't hear me. She's in her room. Door shut. As usual." A little scrap of bitter laughter floated upward. "The news is that she's going to stay on for a while—that is, if Judge Rick agrees to the arrangement—and that's something."

Christina tried to move back up the stairs. But like Cryboy Philawell, whose story had terrified her so as a small child that she'd never dared listen to it again, her feet were slowly turning to stone.

"I might add," Natalie Keller went on, her voice rising with new sharpness, "that under the circumstances, it's the least she could do. If it weren't for her, the Blaises, the Cantwells, and all the other albatrosses that managed to hang themselves around Dave's neck, he would probably be alive today."

Christina stared into the darkness until the conversation was finished then stumbled back to her room.

That night with new guilt lying on her heart, she did not sleep at all. The next morning, it was clear even to Mrs. Keller that she was not well enough to go to school.

Mid-afternoon, Davey opened the door of her bedroom. "I'm home, Chrissie."

Lying on her back in bed, Christina let her eyes flicker in his direction.

"Grandma brought me. She's downstairs."

"That's nice."

"Can I come in?"

There was no need to answer, for Davey was already in. His eyes, level with the top of her dresser, were taking in all her treasures.

"Don't touch anything," she said.

"I wasn't going to, Chrissie."

Rebuked, Christina turned to the wall but still she could feel Davey's presence in the room. Presently, he circled the bed to look at her. "Are you sick?"

The question—childish, sweet, and sympathetic—made

tears come to her eyes and she nodded.

"Sick enough to have the doctor?"

Minutes passed before she answered. "I . . . I'm not that sick. I . . . I'm going to get up now and get dressed. You can tell your mother I'm feeling better."

After he had gone she showered, dressed, put on a little makeup. Better to pretend than have Mrs. Keller call the doctor—particularly, to call a doctor like Dr. Fair.

"I had a depression some years ago," Miss Lamb said. "A rather serious one. So I think I know the signs."

"I don't know what you mean." Christina did not look up. It was enough that Miss Lamb should ask her to stop to see her after school, without looking into those eyes that were so deep and blue that you could drown in them.

"What I mean is, that in the last two weeks you have been absent three times, that the last piece of work you turned in could have been done by my ten-year-old niece, and in class your mind's a hundred miles away. More significant, you are unhappy."

Christina moved uncomfortably. "Nobody's happy all the time."

Miss Lamb seemed not to have heard. "When you're older, Christina," she paused to pick a withered leaf from the plant on her desk, "you'll study a book by Francis Bacon that he called *Novum Organum*. In it, among many other things, he discusses the 'idols,' or fallacies, that corrupt human understanding. The one that always interested me most was *The Idols of the Cave*."

"Cave?" She had responded without meaning to.

"Francis Bacon says that everyone, every individual person, has a cave or den of his own which refracts and discolors the light of nature." Miss Lamb had turned toward her now and was speaking slowly, softly, but so distinctly that each word seemed to fall like a pebble into a still pool. "I was in my cave for rather a long time—until I was willing to accept help from those who wanted to, and could, help me."

Christina turned away. "I don't want to talk about it any more. Talking doesn't help at all."

Clay was waiting in the car. Christina got in without speaking, slumping in an attitude of dejection.

"I hope it wasn't that bad," Clay said with a little smile as he turned the car into the street.

When Christina didn't answer, he tried again. "What happened? What did she want, anyway?"

Christina plucked at a raveling on the blue cover of her notebook. "What happened was that she jumped all over me—about the work I'm doing."

"Couldn't it be, that with everything that has happened, that maybe your work has gone downhill?" Although he chose his words carefully, had made his voice as placatory as possible, the effort served only as an irritant.

"Of course, my work has gone downhill!" Christina cried. "But it's not my fault! When does she think I have time to study? Picking Davey up at school every afternoon, walking home with him because Mrs. Keller thinks he needs the exercise, keeping an eye on him until she gets home from the shop at six o'clock, helping get dinner, doing the dishes while *she* studies, then giving Davey his bath and putting him to bed while she goes off to her shorthand and typing class."

Clay's silence was so disapproving that Christina bit her lip to keep it from trembling. "If you think I'm so terrible, why don't you just come right out and say so?"

"Christina, will you *cut* it?" Clay blasted on the horn as he spoke, giving a squirrel who had just started to cross the street a nervous breakdown.

Frightened, she put her hand on his knee. "Please, Clay. Don't you be cross with me, too. I . . . I can't bear it." Her voice trembled and broke.

"I'm *not* cross with you!" He spoke with such

vehemence that she drew back her hand. "It's just that lately, I don't understand you. And I'm not the only one. Trimble asked me the other day if something was wrong. She said you don't meet her and Trish for lunch in the cafeteria any more."

He was looking at her closely, clinically, "Sometimes, you almost seem like two different people."

"What do you mean?" Her tone was sharp.

Clay swallowed uncomfortably. "Forget it. I didn't mean anything."

"You must have meant something, or you wouldn't have said it." Now she was watching him so narrowly that he flushed.

"I can't explain it. In some ways, you seem grown up. Braver than any girl I've ever known—losing your parents, coming cold into a new school. It's the other you, I don't understand—the only one I seem to be seeing much of, lately. Chris, listen." He took her hand but she jerked it away. Flushing, he continued, "I don't want to make you sorer than you already are, but maybe you should see a doctor—like you were going to do that day that Barb saw you."

Christina felt still inside, cold, as ice. "If you'll just stop the car and let me out . . ."

"I thought we were going to pick Davey up at school."

His very reasonableness, his calm manner like that of a father dealing with an unreasonable child, caused the last shred of her own control to vanish. "You don't care anything about me. You never did. I was just someone to be sorry for—so you could be important."

"If you feel that way, there isn't much point in trying to be friends," Clay said. There was a white line around his lips. "But that still is no reason why I shouldn't drive you and Davey home—on a cold day."

"You needn't bother," she said. "Just stop the car. Please." She was out of the car before the wheels had stopped turning and was running, books clutched to her chest, down the street. She heard the deep-throated growl of Clay's car behind her but he did not come abreast of her and stop.

A hundred heartbeats later when she dared to turn and look, the white convertible was nowhere in sight.

When she reached the school, Davey was waiting in the playground. He got up from the large boulder where he'd been sitting and came jogging toward her across the cindered field. A large crayon drawing buffeted from one mittened hand.

Old tears had dried on his cheeks but they had no power to move her. "Hi, Chrissie." He spoke almost shyly.

"Hi, Davey. I had to stay after school a little. That's why I'm late."

"That's all right, Chrissie."

They began to walk.

"I made a drawing." He handed it halfway toward her but she did not take it. "It's a dinosaur."

"It's very nice."

When the wind whipped it from his mittened fingers and sent it skittering away behind him down the street, she did not notice and only for a moment did he look back. "It wasn't any good anyway," he said.

Christina, deep in her own thoughts, looked up. "What did you say?"

The question, she decided, was not worth an answer for Davey did not reply and the two continued in silence up the street.

A passing bread truck with a large Monarch butterfly painted on its side looked as if it were about to stop and then moved on.

CHAPTER ELEVEN

Toys in the Attic

Somehow she managed to survive the interminable day. Only one thing helped at all. Miss Lamb was not at school to offer unwanted advice—the cold that had been troubling her all week having apparently taken a turn for the worse. In any event, a substitute teacher named Miss Fringle was at Miss Lamb's desk and spent the entire period reading to the class in a nasal voice the Daniel Webster chapter in *Profiles in Courage*.

What was courage? It took courage just to go on living. Courage she was not sure she had. Her hand closed around the bottle of small green pills in her pocket. Waking with a headache early that morning after only an hour or two of troubled sleep, she had been looking for aspirin in the bathroom medicine chest when she found them. Half-hidden behind toothpaste and mouthwash, the bottle would have escaped her attention if it had not been for the strip of paper wrapped around it and the words "Extra Digitalis Tablets for Dave" written on it in Natalie Keller's firm hand.

A moment later, her search for aspirin forgotten, the bottle was in the pocket of her robe. Medicine strong enough to help an ailing heart must be very strong indeed. Padding downstairs to the study, she took the "Damascu to Educ" volume of the encyclopedia from the shelf. And she was right, as she had known she would be.

The knowledge was her only comfort as she walked toward her locker. Her footsteps echoed lonesomely. In the last ten minutes, the building had emptied. Everyone had gone happily home to mothers, fathers, brothers, or sisters. Everyone else had friends. Now that she had lost Clay she had no one. A short, bitter laugh escaped her. She had no one except the fat girl who was standing by her locker.

"I knew you hadn't gone home yet," the fat girl said. "I saw you go into the girls' rest room after the last bell rang. I . . . I was waiting to say good-bye."

Christina turned from her open locker. "Good-*bye?*" There was something about the fat girl's voice that challenged her. "You're going somewhere?"

The fat girl smiled. "You might say that. It's sort of a high point in my life. In any case, I won't be back."

Christina looked at the fat girl and frowned, as one might do while working on a jigsaw puzzle with pieces missing. There *was* something different about her—a kind of assurance, almost a kind of happiness she had never observed in her before. "Well, good-bye, then. Maybe we'll meet again some day." The words were empty, spoken without meaning but the fat girl challenged them. "I doubt that," she smiled again, as if pleased with herself, then said, "Oh, I almost forgot. Here's something for you. You can open it when I'm gone." The plain envelope she gave Christina was sealed and bore no writing.

"Why, thank you," Christina said. She turned the envelope over as if another glance might reveal what was inside, then put it between the pages of her history book. When she looked up the fat girl was walking swiftly down the hall.

For a moment it occurred to her that it might be interesting to find out what the fat girl was like inside. She could call after her and suggest that they, at least, walk as far as Davey's school together. The moment was lost, however, in the immensity of her own self-interest. She waited until the fat girl had time to leave the building before she, herself, started out.

A station wagon was parked in front of Davey's school. As Christina neared, a front window was rolled down and Liz Printemps boomed out, "I've got Davey inside. Hop in and I'll drive you home. It's getting colder by the minute."

Not only was Davey inside, but the two younger Printemps children and several of their friends. In the confusing ride that followed, Christina was sure that Mrs. Printemps could not have noticed her silence.

Davey disappeared as soon as they were in the house and she went to the kitchen to read the note that Mrs. Keller had left propped up on the kitchen counter. "Scrub three potatoes for baking. Make meat loaf (Recipe in file). Scrape carrots."

As if they were separate entities, her hands performed the tasks while her mind followed its tortuous turnings. Miss Stevenson's monthly visit was only three days away. She had no hope of pulling herself together. Miss Stevenson would only have to look at her to know that her world had collapsed again. If that were not enough, she would need only talk to Miss Lamb or any other of her teachers to know that since Dave Keller's death her work had gone steadily downhill. Even Mrs. Keller no longer needed her, for Mrs. Basset, the favored baby-sitter, had returned from California and was now available. Davey, himself, could not care less.

So deep was she in thought that a little later when Davey came to the kitchen door and asked her something, she had to ask him to repeat.

"Does Mommy have to go to school again tonight?"

She answered yes, not asking why, and the house was silent again.

When the knock sounded at the front door, minutes passed before she went to answer it and her "Who's there?" sounded so strange in her ears that it might have been spoken in a foreign tongue.

Yet only a second later, a voice answered. "Telephone Company. I'm answering a service call."

"There isn't anything the matter with our phone," she said through the closed door. She turned to look at the phone, sitting silently on the table behind her. But there *could* be, she thought. The phone had not rung since she'd got home from school. Mrs. Keller would be angry, understandably so, if she'd called for a serviceman and then Christina had refused to let him in.

"Don't panic," Leo Cole said. "I had to see you. It was the only way . . ."

If he had made any move to touch her, she would have screamed. Even so, she could feel her mouth form the shape of a cry though no sound came.

"I don't work for the Telephone Company. That's a lie. If I hadn't lied you wouldn't have opened the door. But I do have a job. Driving a bread truck. Butterfly bread. Maybe you've seen me . . . driving around . . . trying to get up nerve . . ."

She remembered now. Once she'd seen the bread truck in the park. And only yesterday, walking home from school . . .

"I was afraid to stop and try to talk to you for fear I'd frighten you . . . that you'd run away, like you did that day I waited for you outside the drugstore. I can't say I blame you—after the way I acted when you were living with Aunt Hen . . ."

She knew his eyes were seeking hers as he talked, but when she neither answered nor returned his gaze he struggled on. "I'm not much . . . I never was and I don't want to make myself out any better than I am, but it's the God's truth I never did mean to hurt you. Why, when I first heard you were coming to stay with Aunt Hen I was nut enough to think that the two of us might be friends. Go to a movie now and then, swim at the beach. Friends! With you! What a laugh!" A short, bitter sound that was more like a sob than a laugh burst from his lips. "You thought I was dirt. I . . . I hated you. So I bugged you. After your dad was killed, I was ashamed. But there wasn't any way to undo what I'd done. I felt like a louse the night I heard you go down to Aunt Hen's room and come back crying, but when you left the house—I was afraid. There wasn't anything else to do but follow you."

"If you hadn't . . ." Christina put her face in her hands.

Leo Cole shrugged. "Don't give me more credit than I deserve. If it hadn't been for me, maybe you'd never have left the house that night at all. Maybe you'd never even have thought about going to the lake. Maybe you'd have turned back and got to the shore without me. Who knows? The shore patrol said you were still swimming strong and easy when they reached you."

"I . . . I don't know," Christina said. "After I left Aunt Henriette's house I don't remember anything at all." She pressed her fingers hard against her eyes as if the act would clear her inner vision, then looked at Leo Cole. Really seeing him, she could not look away. Not that any dramatic change had taken place. His complexion was still bad. His hair, though not worn as long as she remembered it, was still stringy. His eyes, with their heavy lids and pale blue irises had not changed. But something had. A shadow of a disturbing thought crossed her mind. Perhaps, before, she had only seen in Leo Cole what she *wanted* to see and not what was really there—a lost, seeking person like herself.

He began backing away from the still open door as he spoke. "I've got to be going. I've got a lot of my route to cover before six o'clock. Call Aunt Hen sometime. She's not really such a bad old girl."

Christina watched the bread truck with the big Monarch butterfly painted on its side back down the drive and disappear. She shut the door. *Aunt Hen,* she thought. Anyone called Aunt *Hen* could not be half the ogre of one called Henriette.

The house had grown chilly with the front door open and the thermostat had clicked on. The hum of the furnace was the only sound in the silent house. Where was Davey? What was he doing? She began to ascend the stairs, pausing to listen with each step.

She called out, "Davey!" but when he did not answer an unreasoning apprehension filled her that was not allayed when she reached his room. Disordered, yet strangely empty-looking. Her alarm grew. Could he have run away? Could he have left the house by the back door as she'd stood talking to Leo Cole?

A muffled thump from overhead sent her running down the hall to the stairs that led to the attic. She began to climb, one hand pressing against the cold plaster wall, peering at the square of gray light at the top of the steep flight of stairs. The sounds were clearer now and she called out, "Davey!" once again. But not until she was standing in the attic, accustoming her eyes to the gloom, did she see the little figure moving among the shadows, a bag of blocks too heavy for him to carry, dragging along behind him.

"Davey! What are you doing? It's too dark to play up here!" Her voice was sharp with relief as she picked her way toward him among the cobwebbed objects. She winced as her ankle struck a small sharp object. A fire engine of Davey's, lying on its side, a favorite toy. As she leaned over to right it, she saw Mr. Hawkins. Wrapped in a piece of old blanket he lay staring at the ceiling with his shoe-button eyes.

"Mr. Hawkins . . . your fire truck . . . Lincoln logs . . . little cars . . . all your toys . . . everything." She spread her hands helplessly as she looked about her. Everything he valued had been dragged up the attic stairs and dumped.

"Toys aren't any good without a father," Davey said.

His voice coming out of the now near-darkness, was high and clear, the words as precisely spoken as if they had been memorized, ". . . *or* a mother, or *somebody*."

"You have me." She would not have known that she had spoken—and for her, at that time, so strange and incongruous was the thought that she could not have been sure she had—if a small demon had not come surging toward her. Fists flailing, he struck out blindly as he passed her. "You're not any good to anybody, not to anybody in the whole wide world."

He stood poised at the top of the stairs, took one—perhaps two steps before he fell, tumbling over and over like a disjointed doll until he at last lay motionless in the hall below.

When the telephone rang, Christina crossed to it like a sleepwalker, lifted the receiver and made a small nameless sound.

"The doctor says he's going to be all right," Natalie Keller said, and then broke into tears.

Scarcely breathing, simply existing in a state of thankfulness, Christina waited until Mrs. Keller could go on.

"A slight concussion. The doctor wants to keep him here a few days for observation, then he must be quiet at home for a while." She paused when her breath caught, then went on. "Christina, you . . . you're all right?"

"I'm all right, now." Although Mrs. Keller had refused to allow her to accept the blame for the accident, it would have been meaningless if Davey were not going to be all right.

"Don't wait for me to come home. I feel better here . . . close to him."

Christina hung up the receiver then moving lightly, as if suspended in space, she went upstairs and down the long hall. She found a light switch that turned on a small bulb in the attic stairway. In the attic, a long string dangling

127

from a cord turned on another pale beacon.

An hour later she had all of Davey's belongings back in his room, his bookcase and toy shelves ordered. If it had taken her this long, how long had it taken Davey? How many trips and over how many days? All the time she had been unknowing, so wrapped up in her own misery that she had not heard the sound of one small heart breaking.

Like a tape recorder, her memory played back what Clay had said soon after Dave Keller died and her world, so recently righted, had collapsed again. "Sure, you've got problems. Every kid has. My mother says that most of them begin with 'p.' Peers, parents, poverty, and just plain pressures. You name 'em, and some kid's got them. It . . . it's how they handle them that counts." He'd paused uncomfortably, stammered a little because he seemed to be lecturing, then because he was so honest, he'd stumbled on to finish. "Almost anyone can manage when everything's going his way. The test comes in learning to accept frustration—to be able to manage when everything starts going wrong. . . ." Then he had stopped because she, unwilling to listen, had turned away.

She knew now that Clay was right about kids and their problems. Leo Cole, for instance, living with a troubled conscience—about her. Mitzi, who'd been afraid to love. Davey, coping with the loss of his father and the disruption of his life before he'd reached his seventh birthday. The fat girl, rejected by her parents, whom she would never see again.

The words "never see again" had an ugly, final note. Christina got her books from the hall. The letter the fat girl had given her protruded an inch or so from her history, just as she had placed it. Her fingers fumbled as she tore open the envelope and took out the single, folded sheet torn from a stenographic notebook. A poem, it was written legibly and carefully indented.

"Good creatures, do you love your lives
And have you ears for sense?
Here is a knife like other knives
That cost me eighteen pence.

"I need but stick it in my heart
And down will come the sky
And earth's foundations will depart
And all you folk will die."

A.E. HOUSMAN

She read it once, then again, its meaning nagging at her like a hidden pain.

She had felt that way after her father died. Angry at the world, angry at herself, she had thought mistakenly that by destroying herself that she could destroy the world and all the other persons in it. Could the fat girl, a girl whose name she did not even know, feel like that now? Possibly—but far more likely, Christina tried to reassure herself, the fat girl was safely home in bed, reading poetry and eating a candy bar.

Still, the way to find out would be to call her—and friendly Trimble who knew everyone would know her name.

Trimble, answering the phone, sounded surprised and pleased when Christina explained the purpose of her call. She answered promptly. "Diana Something. Begins with an M . . . I've got it . . . Midgely."

"I wanted to get in touch with her."

Trimble said, "Oh," too polite to sound surprised.

"Maybe I'll see you at school."

"At lunch," Trimble said as smoothly as if nothing had ever interrupted their friendship. "We still have dibs on the same table in the cafeteria."

Christina scarcely heard. With her free hand she had found the "M's" in the pages of the telephone directory but had to go through them again after Trimble hung up before finding the Midgelys' number.

A boy answered Christina's call with an abrupt "Not here" when she asked to speak to Diana.

"When . . . when are you expecting her?"

There was a moment's silence at the other end of the line before she could hear the boy bawling, "Hey! Mom! When's Did coming home?" then say into the receiver, "Don't know."

"But has she come home from school? I mean, has she been home since . . . since morning?"

"Hey! What is this?" the boy said suspiciously. "Who wants to know, anyway?"

The telephone receiver began slipping greasily in Christina's moist hand. The boy must not hang up now, not until she found out what she had to know. "My name's Christina. . . ." She had always had her ways. They came back to her. "I'm a friend of your sister's at school," she said invitingly.

"Yeah?" His suspicion was ebbing. "Wait, I'll ask Mom."

This time he did not bellow but left the phone to find out the answer and when he returned answered civilly. "Nope, not been home since morning."

"Thanks awfully," she said, still breathily. "Good-bye."

Christina tore at a bit of cuticle with her teeth.

Where had Diana Midgely, the fat girl, gone? What had she done after leaving school that afternoon? Blood began to seep through the torn flesh of her finger but she neither noticed it nor felt the pain as she tried to put herself into the body of the fat girl, tried to look at the world through her eyes. If I were she, she thought, where would I go? What would I do? She shivered convulsively, drew her sweater more tightly about her. Clay had not understood, and she could not explain, why she had made him turn around and go the other way the day he had started to take her for a drive on the lake-shore road.

Had there been a clue in the conversation when she had

talked to the fat girl—to Diana Midgely—after school that afternoon?

"You're going somewhere?" she had asked, and the fat girl had smiled. Without trying, Christina could see the way she looked as without trying she could hear what she had said. "It's a high point in my life . . . in any case, I won't be back."

"High Point." Now it was Clay's voice that she heard. "Every couple of years some nut climbs out on the other side of the barrier and jumps . . . nothing but rocks below . . ."

"No! No, not that!" She cried the words aloud, although there was no one to hear. She threw herself face down on the sofa, though there was no one to see. Desperately, she willed her tears—the old refuge for life's impossibilities—to come. But nothing happened. Perhaps, since Davey's fall when she had crouched at the foot of the attic stairs, holding his waxy face close to hers, seeking but not finding the smallest pulse, her tears had been used up. Perhaps, during the interminable minutes that she had waited for Liz Printemps, whom she had frantically called, and Mrs. Keller to arrive, her supply of tears had become exhausted and she would never weep again.

The grandfather clock in the hall struck nine. Portentous as the voice of doom it echoed through the silent house. Five hours had passed since Diana Midgely had handed her the white envelope. It would not take that many hours for Diana to walk to High Point. It could already be too late. Only a person with a car would stand a chance of reaching her before . . .

Christina got up from the sofa, stood listening to the magnified beating of her heart. Wasn't it Dave Keller, himself, who had said, "One of these days I'll let you have a go at Portia"?

CHAPTER TWELVE

Begin Again

The car keys were hanging on a nail in the kitchen hallway, a cardboard disc labeled "Portia" was next to a St. Christopher medal on the chain.

She had not seen the green car, nor thought about it since Dave Keller died. Nor had it, obviously, been driven. Her gloveless hands grew colder still as the motor turned over and over before finally igniting, then with a whispered "good girl" she turned the car into the street.

But if Portia was "good," it took Christina less than twenty minutes of driving to know that she was not. Whether because of the unfamiliarity of the old car, her own lack of experience driving any car, or the tenseness that had been building up within her, her sense of direction failed when she reached the area where she knew she should turn off for the High Point road.

Afraid to waste more time, she turned into a filling station blazing with lights and plastic pennants fluttering noisily in the November wind. A boy in a clean coverall came out. She cranked down the window of the car. "How do I get to High Point?"

"Two blocks straight ahead to the stoplight, then one to the right. You can't miss . . ." He stopped abruptly as if her unsteady voice, her appearance—gloveless hands, her only wrap a sweater—had just registered, "What do you want to go there for, at this time of night?"

Her lip trembled. He had no right to question her. Or, in this mixed-up brother's keeper's world (why else had Leo Cole followed her?) perhaps he did. "I . . . I'm meeting a friend."

The attendant, his hand resting on the open window, was looking at her. He was older than she'd thought, not a boy at all. He wore a wedding ring. "I don't know who this friend is you're meeting, kiddo, but if I were you, I'd cool it."

She drove off quickly, not thanking him. Through the rear-view mirror she could see him watching her as she waited for a string of cars to pass.

"Two blocks down. One to the right." The words kept repeating themselves in her mind even after she was safely on the High Point road. The curves seemed to grow sharper and the road narrower as she continued. Once she killed the engine. In restarting it and releasing the handbrake, the car moved sickeningly backward. Perspiration broke on her forehead and despite the cold her gloveless hands were clammy with moisture. If the car had crashed through the guardrail, she knew what people— Judge Rick, Miss Stevenson, Miss Lamb, perhaps even Clay—would think. And they would think wrong. So very wrong. A fragment of poetry by Robert Frost came unbidden to her mind.

> "The woods are lovely, dark and deep,
> But I have promises to keep,
> And miles to go before I sleep. . . ."

Before the car had come to a stop, she saw the dark huddled figure on the bench.

"Diana?" she spoke softly, moving toward her. "It's Christy."

The figure did not turn. "I thought maybe you'd come."

"Because . . . because of the poem?"

"That, maybe. Maybe because I . . . I needed somebody so much. Needed somebody to *look* at me . . . to *see* me."

"I see you now," Christina said. Strange, because even the scrap of moon that earlier had hung in the sky had now disappeared. Below them, mist had blotted out the lights of the city. Darkness enclosed them.

The fat girl moved bulkily on the bench, making room for Christina. "But you needn't have worried. It . . . it was just an idea. I . . . I've thought things out. I couldn't do anything so silly. Still, I'm glad you came."

"If you're ready to go, I'll drive you home," Christina said.

"I suppose I might as well, even if my dad does skin me alive." She laughed wryly. "Some job. Skinning *me*."

"If your dad didn't love you, he wouldn't care what you did."

"I suppose. But it's a funny way to show someone you care."

They were both in the car but Christina had not yet managed to turn it around when the patrol car appeared. "Everything all right up here?"

Christina blinked in the sudden brief glare of a flashlight. "Y . . . yes, sir. We're just leaving."

The police car was still following at a discreet distance when Christina let Diana out in front of her house. Nor did it blink its headlights in friendly farewell until she had turned on a light in the Kellers' living room to prove that she was safely inside.

Ravenously hungry for the first time in days, Christina went to the kitchen and made a pan of cocoa. Sitting at the kitchen table she drank two cups—Mrs. Keller would enjoy the rest when she got home from the hospital—and ate two pieces of buttered toast with cinnamon and sugar on top.

She was filled with a feeling so strange that for awhile she could not give it a name. Satisfaction. In spite of everything that had happened, it had been a good day. The little green pills lay scattered, where she had hurled them, on the rocks below High Point. Even the arrival of the police car as they were leaving had been good because it proved that the filling-station attendant had cared about the welfare of a girl he had never seen before and would never see again. The police car, however, *had* had one disadvantage. With it following her she had had to drive so cautiously that she'd hardly dared to talk to Diana at all. She would have liked to tell her more about the five "p's"—Diana's "p" was most obviously parents—and to explain that all *kids* had problems and that it was the way you handled them that counted. Life wasn't very complicated when you had everything you wanted at the very minute you wanted it. The test came in learning to accept the stupid frustrations that came along. To function reasonably well when things went wrong.

Christina smiled to herself. Perhaps it was just as well she *hadn't* had a chance to tell Diana all of that. It was one thing to mouth a philosophy, another thing to practice it. There'd be time to improve Diana after she had been to see Dr. Fair.

Christina opened the door to which she had been directed, then took a diffident step backward. "I had an appointment with Dr. Fair."

Behind the desk the woman in the pale blue knit suit smiled. "I'm Dr. Fair. The M.E. stands for Mary Elizabeth. It is rather sneaky of me, I'm afraid, to hide behind my initials and my maiden name. But it has its advantages."

136

Christina moved into the room, circling lightly, as a small creature might do in a strange environment. Pots of ivy flourished on a window ledge. There were paintings on the walls—several watercolors, a small oil, and a number of prints she vaguely recognized. On the desk was a family photograph—a father, mother (a younger Dr. Fair), and four look-alike, vaguely familiar children.

Back at the window, she looked down at the people moving about on the sidewalk below. Bodies foreshortened, shoulders thrust forward, armed with bundles, briefcases, shopping bags, each person was moving directly or indirectly, purposefully or aimlessly toward his destiny.

She turned back into the room, sat down in the nearest chair. "Where do you want me to begin?"

"Wherever you like. It doesn't really matter."

"Don't tell her anything," the girl inside spoke shrilly, insisting to be heard. "At any rate, don't tell her about *me.*"

"Oh, be quiet," Christina said, half-aloud. "I'll tell her what I like." So she did. After all Dr. Fair was waiting, and the unhappy history of the girl inside seemed a good place to begin.

Walking toward her locker, Christina saw Clay coming toward her. Her face burned with embarrassment and anxiety. She had not seen him to talk to since the day they had quarreled. She corrected herself. Since *she* had quarreled with *him.* She could not blame him if he never talked to her again.

Clay jogged to a stop. "I've been incommunicado for a week. Boning up for College Board exams." He grinned. "I'm not sure but what I'm boning up too late. Still, it may help some."

"I've missed you, Clay," she said. It was nice to speak the truth and good to see him smile.

"I've missed you, too, Christy. I was wondering if I might drive you home."

"If we could take Diana Midgely. . . . Lately, I've been walking home with her."

"Sure thing," Clay said, with less than enthusiasm. "But I'd been sort of hoping we might have a chance to talk. I . . . I haven't been very happy since I saw you last."

"Maybe you could come in afterward for a little while. But I do have to go straight home. A baby-sitter's there with Davey. He's not out of the hospital very long. He . . . he had a fall." So much had happened that Clay did not know about.

"No kidding? That's rough on the little guy. And Mrs. Keller too. She's had her troubles all right."

"Oh, there's Diana now." She turned to greet her. "Hi! Diana, this is Clay Harger—Diana Midgely. Or do you two know each other?"

"I know *him*," said Diana Midgely. If her tone was not sullen, it still left no doubt of the impression she wished to convey.

"Clay'll drive us home."

"Not me. I've got to go downtown to see some dumb psychologist. Miss Greenlie's trapped me into seeing him."

"It's not Dr. Wheat, is it?"

Diana looked so astonished that Christina laughed. "He's really not bad at all. Though I'm afraid I gave him a rather bad time."

"*You* know him?"

"I was at the Juvenile Home for a while before I came to live with the Kellers." It was strange, Christina thought, that this piece of information long withheld and so carefully concealed, should have slipped out so easily. Strange, too, that Diana Midgely—gross, fat, so long scorned—had the delicacy to ignore it.

"Thanks anyway. For the ride, I mean. But even if I were going home, I'd walk." She looked down at her shapeless self with a sly smile. "O! that this too too solid flesh would melt," she intoned. "Thaw and resolve itself into a dew . . ."

138

Clay laughed. Christina smiled, thinking of Mitzi. If she and Diana knew each other, they could quote poetry all day. And all night, too.

"There's more, you know," said Diana, still with the same sly, smile.

"Or that the Everlasting had not fix'd
His canon 'gainst self-slaughter! O God! O God!
How weary, stale, flat and unprofitable
Seem to me all the uses of this world."

Finished, she grinned wickedly. "Poor Hamlet! What a depressive! But who knows? If he'd had somebody like Dr. Wheat to go to, he might be alive today." She slammed her locker door shut smartly. "See you Monday," she said, and was gone as silently as she had come.

Snow was falling when Clay and Christina got outside. Great, wet flakes that clung to their coats, clogged the anxious blades of the windshield wipers. Clay stopped once to scrape off the snow on the rear window.

"You look as if you'd been dipped in frosting," Christina said when he got back in. "Coconut."

Clay shook his head, sending crystals of water dancing.

Christina looked out the window. "I've been to a doctor since I saw you last. Twice. A psychiatrist."

"I know," Clay said. He sat very straight at the wheel, looking ahead into the swirling whiteness. "My mother told me you'd been to see her. She said she didn't think it would matter if you knew. Honest relationships between people are always best."

"Your mother is Dr. Fair." It was a statement, not really a question, and she made it without resentment, without too much surprise. "Did you know that's where I was going that day that Barb Jethrow saw me?"

"I guessed. Later on, when I found out about your parents everything went together."

The car slithered sidewise as it turned in the Keller

drive, then plowed ahead, pulling in beside Mrs. Basset's car under the protection of the porte cochere.

"Will the baby-sitter be afraid to drive home?" Clay asked. "I could take her."

"Not Mrs. Basset. She's indomitable. She drove home by herself from California."

The baby-sitter was, however, waiting just inside the front door, ready to go. "Davey's been fine, just fine," she said. "A little difficult, but when a child begins to act ornery it's a sure sign he's getting well."

Davey was sitting like a king in his father's big chair in the study. A wedding-ring quilt, made by some great-aunt, wrapped the lower part of his body mummy-fashion. The breadboard from the kitchen was placed across the arms of the chair to form a desk.

"What are we going to do now?" Davey cried. Two spots of color as round and red as if they had been applied artificially, burned in his cheeks.

"Nothing," Christina said firmly from the hall where she was taking off her coat. "Nothing at all. Except to talk quietly. I think you've about had it for one day."

Clay had already walked into the study where Davey sat. "Hi, Coach." He held out his hand.

Davey shook it. "I'm not a coach," he said. "Yet." He grinned, reconsidering. "Yes, I am, too. Coach for the Green Bay Packers."

"Hey, listen to that!" Clay called out, not aware that Christina had entered the book-lined room. "Pretty sharp. How old is this kid, anyway?"

"Six," Christina said, in a voice that was a mixture of pride and exasperation. The more time she spent with Davey, the more she felt like his mother.

What his mother felt like, she didn't know. Dr. Fair said that if the problems kids had weren't solved when they were kids, they carried them over into adulthood. Mrs. Keller probably had some of those. As who didn't? Sometimes, Christina worried about Davey.

He had started to use his crayons in a coloring book. The tip of his tongue held tight between his teeth was red as a strawberry. "I'm going to marry Chrissie when I'm big."

"If I were you, Coach," Clay said, "I wouldn't be too sure of that. Somebody will probably beat you to it."

Most likely, Christina thought. She looked at Clay and smiled. Most *very* likely. But later. After she'd given the girl inside time to grow up. . . .

Mrs. Basset had brought in the mail, left it on the end of the desk. Christina leafed through it, not really looking for anything for herself but rather as an excuse to listen to Clay and Davey talk.

Bills, circulars, personal letters for Mrs. Keller—even after a month, letters of sympathy continued to come in from people Dave Keller had aided. Frequently, they were from people about whom his wife had never heard. But, at least, her bitterness was vanishing. Often she wept when she read this mail. And now that the two of them were learning to be friends, she sometimes shared parts of letters with Christina. "He was so good," she once said. "He never said to anyone who asked his help, 'What does this have to do with me?' "

At the very bottom of the pile of mail, Christina found the letter addressed to her. Postmarked Sea Island, Georgia, she looked at it curiously. Who could be writing to her from there? Indeed, who could be writing to her at all? Other than letters from the attorney for her father's estate in Spring Valley, no mail came her way—not even a "pretend" letter from Karachi, which she no longer needed now that she was better.

The letter in her hand had been sent airmail. And the writing looked familiar. The paper crackled expensively as she found an unsealed spot in the flap of the envelope. Inserting a forefinger, she opened it and drew out a sheet of matching paper.

"Dear L.M. of Astolat:

Remember me and that rich old lady I used to talk about adopting me? Well, she has. It's not legal yet but the machinery is in motion. We'll be here in Sea Island where I'm in school for another month then we're coming back home. How do you like that? *Home.* Her name is Mrs. Grandrath. She's sweet—not really so old, either—and until she met me she was embittered over the loss of her only child. Can you believe it???? Write, if the notion ever seizes you.

Love,
Eva

"P.S. If you're wondering what happened to 'Mitzi,' the truth is that Mrs. G. has a poodle by that name and one of us had to give. Oh, well. A small price to pay for living happily ever after. After all,
'What's in a name? That which we call a rose
By any other name would smell as sweet.'

Romeo and Juliet, Act II, Scene 2
E."

(Please turn page)

A DATE FOR DIANE
by Betty Cavanna   (X2198-60¢)

LOVE LAURIE
by Betty Cavanna   (F1221-50¢)

ALMOST LIKE SISTERS
by Betty Cavanna   (F1397-50¢)

MEET THE MALONES
by Betty Cavanna   (F1458-50¢)

BEANY HAS A SECRET LIFE
by Betty Cavanna   (X2201-60¢)

SENIOR PROM
by Rosamond du Jardin   (F1219-50¢)

THE REAL THING
by Rosamond du Jardin   (X2031-60¢)

MARCY CATCHES UP
by Rosamond du Jardin   (F1120-50¢)

Send for a free list of all our books in print

These books are available at your local newsstand, or send price indicated plus 15¢ per copy to cover mailing costs, to Berkley Publishing Corporation, 200 Madison Avenue, New York, N.Y. 10016